"Grateful

demanded Elsabeth.

"You're seriously suggesting I'd go to bed with you out of *gratitude?* You think I don't know my own feelings better than that? Not to mention value myself? Why you—"

Briggs took a prudent step backward and grinned at her. "Go ahead, let it all out. You'll feel better."

"I will not! Don't you tell me how I'll feel. I'm *grateful* when the mailman realizes I didn't put enough postage on a letter and fixes it for me. I'm *grateful* when somebody brings me something special for my garden. I'm *grateful* for shared recipes and birthday presents and phone calls from old friends. I am *not* grateful for having my existence turned upside down, for being scared out of my wits and for not knowing if I'm coming or going because some dumb cop from Bridgeport is living in my guest room and messing up my head!"

Dear Reader,

When two people fall in love, the world is suddenly new and exciting, and it's that same excitement we bring to you in Silhouette Intimate Moments. These are stories with scope and grandeur. The characters lead lives we all dream of, and everything they do reflects the wonder of being in love.

Longer and more sensuous than most romances, Silhouette Intimate Moments novels take you away from everyday life and let you share the magic of love. Adventure, glamour, drama, even suspense— these are the passwords that let you into a world where love has a power beyond the ordinary, where the best authors in the field today create stories of love and commitment that will stay with you always.

In coming months, look for novels by your favorite authors: Heather Graham Pozzessere, Emilie Richards and Kathleen Korbel, to name just a few. And whenever you buy books, look for all the Silhouette Intimate Moments, love stories for today's woman by today's woman.

Leslie J. Wainger
Senior Editor and Editorial Coordinator

MAURA SEGER

Caught in the Act

SILHOUETTE·INTIMATE·MOMENTS®

Published by Silhouette Books New York

America's Publisher of Contemporary Romance

SILHOUETTE BOOKS
300 East 42nd St., New York, N.Y. 10017

CAUGHT IN THE ACT

ISBN: 0-373-07389-5

First Silhouette Books printing July 1991

Printed in the U.S.A.

Books by Maura Seger

Silhouette Intimate Moments

Silver Zephyr #61
Golden Chimera #96
Comes A Stranger #108
Shadows of the Heart #137
Quest of the Eagle #149
Dark of the Moon #162
Happily Ever After #176
Legacy #194
Sea Gate #209
Day and Night #224
Conflict of Interest #236
Unforgettable #253
Change of Plans #280
Painted Lady #342
Caught in the Act #389

Silhouette Books

Silhouette Christmas Stories 1986
"Starbright"

Silhouette Desire

Cajun Summer #282
Treasure Hunt #295

Silhouette Special Edition

A Gift Beyond Price #135

MAURA SEGER

was prompted by a love of books and a vivid imagination to decide, at age twelve, to be a writer. Twenty years later, her first book was published. So much, she says, for overnight success! Now each book is an adventure filled with fascinating people who always surprise her.

Chapter 1

Elsabeth Grace couldn't find her thumb. She'd looked everywhere for it but with no luck. Worse yet, she was going to be late for work. Not that it made much sense showing up without her thumb. She couldn't work without it.

"Now where the heck...?" she murmured as she plowed under a heap of pillows on the old couch in front of the fireplace. The clock was ticking. Meanwhile, she had a ten-mile drive to the restaurant and needed time to get into her costume and...

"*Ah-ha.*" There it was, nestled in a crack between two cushions. Her thumb. Or, more correctly, thumb tip. That all-purpose, absolutely essential prop no magician would be without. Perfect for squirreling away silk scarves, colorful flags and shakersful of salt, small glasses of water and so on.

"Zared," Elsabeth murmured under her breath. The silver-gray cat of the same name—although he frequently refused to acknowledge it—blinked at her from his perch on the back of the couch.

"You have to stop doing this," she said reproachfully. "Leave my stuff alone."

Zared blinked again, turned his head and began to wash. Typical. A cat would never admit to anything. He certainly wouldn't tell how he had managed to get into the latched case Elsabeth used for storing magic equipment. Someday she was going to catch him at it, and then . . .

But that was for later; right now she had to get to work. She hurried out of the house, shut the door behind her and remembered to lock it. Redding, Connecticut, might be a long way from the big city, but crime could crop up anywhere, and there was no sense taking chances.

Her car was waiting in the driveway. It was a very old, very battered Ford that should have been totally lacking in character or distinction. Yet somehow it had managed to acquire both, along with the most ornery temperament she had ever encountered in a mechanical device, presuming that was actually what it was. While stalled on the interstate one day early on in their relationship, she had dubbed the car Beelzebub. The name fit.

She turned the key in the ignition and listened to the engine cough and sputter as usual. Having stated its objections to going anywhere, it grudgingly started up.

The sun was setting as she drove away from the two-story saltbox house painted a cheerful barn red. She glanced back at it in the rearview mirror, feeling as she always did the pleasant start of surprise and gratitude that the house was really hers. From the first time she had seen it as a small child, she had loved the house. Quiet, simple and filled with tantalizing surprises, it had always seemed the most marvelous of places. Totally unlike the succession of hotel rooms and efficiency apartments she had shared with her parents until going away to college.

Great-aunt Georgette had understood all that. With her death at the age of eighty the previous year, the house had come to Elsabeth. Since then she had left it only briefly to work. All the rest of her time had been spent on the refurbishing that an elderly woman like Georgette had necessarily let go. In particular, she was restoring the garden to its former glory.

On this warm summer evening, she could smell the honeysuckle, which had been coaxed to grow along trellises beside the kitchen windows. A few industrious bees still buzzed around the roses, and the last of the squirrels was on its way home. Tomorrow she would need to weed the borders again and mulch the flowerbeds. But first things first.

The Red Rooster Inn was a new restaurant trying hard to look old. Installed in a renovated barn not far from the highway, it appealed to city dwellers in search of a country fix. Lately there seemed to be an awful lot of them. The parking lot was almost full when Elsabeth drove up. She left Beelzebub around the back and went in through the kitchen entrance.

Hermione was checking the salad supplies. She looked up, saw Elsabeth and sighed with relief. "Thank God, we thought you weren't coming. Mike's spitting hairs."

Hermione was always saying things like that. Elsabeth had no idea what they meant—spitting hairs?—but that didn't bother her. There was a great deal she didn't understand.

"Sorry, I got hung up." She flashed the large, blond girl a smile and hurried through the kitchen to the tiny cubbyhole Mike—the Inn's proprietor—had set aside as a dressing room when he had decided a little entertainment for the restaurant wouldn't hurt. Little was the key word. The size of the cubbyhole required Mike to hire only solo acts, which was fine with him. Entertainment was entertainment, and solo was usually the cheapest.

Not that there was anything cheap about Elsabeth. Mike would be the first to admit that she was a class act. She thought of that as she looked at herself in the cracked mirror that took up most of one wall. She wore the traditional black tie and tails of the professional magician, only in her case they were tailored to a figure that seemed to have more curves than straight lines.

She had, as her mother had always said, blossomed early. At thirty-one she was tall, on the slender side without overdoing it, and unlikely to ever be mistaken for anything other than female. A heart-shaped face, delicate features, large azure eyes and flyaway russet hair completed the picture. Her looks had caused occasional problems, but over the years she'd learned just the right combination of deadpan patter and drop-dead look it took to convince any would-be masher that it wouldn't be worth the effort.

Still, she was glad to have left the big city with its big

city habits for the far quieter life of a small Connecticut town. Everything was so much calmer and safer here. People were more civilized, more polite, much saner and—what was that out there behind the Inn? A scream?

No, it couldn't be. People in Connecticut didn't scream. They kept their voices nice and low, smooth, like water that had never had a rock tossed in it. She had to be imagining things.

"Aaagh!"

That definitely sounded like a scream. Gingerly she propped open the tiny window and peered out into the darkness. The back of the Inn was lit, as law required, near the exit, but the illumination didn't reach very far. Just enough for her to see the shapes of four men struggling beside a car.

Instinctively she reached out a hand and flipped off the dressing room light. Standing in the darkness, she could see better. There were definitely four men, all dressed in business suits. Three were much larger than the one they seemed to be forcing into the car.

"Hey!" she yelled in a deliberately non-Connecticut voice that could have reached most of the way to Indiana. "What do you think you're doing?"

The men froze, all except for their heads, which swiveled in every direction as they tried to locate the voice. Satisfied she had gained a few moments, Elsabeth was about to run from the dressing room to alert Mike when a car passing on the side road suddenly shone its headlights into the back lot. For an instant she could clearly see the faces of all four men.

And clearly hear them.

"Damn!"

"Come on!"

"Move it! Let's go!"

She was through the dressing room door in a flash, running flat-out into the kitchen.

"Somebody's being kidnapped! Get Mike! Get the police!"

Hermione stared at her, mouth open, big brown eyes wide as saucers. "What the kittens . . . ?"

Elsabeth didn't wait to explain but shoved through the door and raced into the back lot in time to hear the squeal of tires and see the car pulling away. Dimly she could make out the face of the fourth man in the backseat, his features pale and contorted with fear.

"Damn," she said fervently under her breath.

"Damn what?" Mike demanded. He was a large, burly man with sandy hair, a blunt-instrument face and ham-sized hands that were wrapped competently around a double-barreled shotgun.

"Black four-door sedan," Elsabeth said. "Connecticut plates, WR9-something. Three men snatched a fourth. Call the police!"

"You okay?" he asked.

"I'm fine. That man . . ."

"It's okay," Mike said, lowering the shotgun. "The cops are on their way."

The call came in just before Detective Brigham Caldwell was due to quit for the night. He was looking forward to it. The boredom of his present assignment was driving him—to put it politely—around the bend. He was a peaceful, orderly man by nature—hence his profession—but he was willing to admit that he was desperate for a little diversion. Out here in

God's country, there didn't seem to be much difference between being on duty or off. Absolutely nothing happened.

All right, not absolutely. Yesterday they'd picked up a couple of kids for speeding and found a gram of coke in the glove compartment. When he was on drug detail in Bridgeport, he'd figured busts in kilos, not grams. Grams hardly registered on the scale of big-city crime, but out here they were taken far more seriously, as two dumb-punk kids were now learning the hard way.

Out here. He twitched slightly, trying not to listen to the hum of the tree frogs coming from the other side of the window. Last night, on the way back to civilization, he'd seen a deer standing in the center of somebody's front lawn not twenty feet from the main road. It had raised its head, looked at him calmly and gone back to munching whatever expensive ornamental shrub it had decided looked tasty.

In Bridgeport, where Briggs was supposed to be and would have been were it not for a truly monumental bureaucratic screwup, the deer wouldn't have lasted two minutes. Out here it seemed to think it owned the place.

He sighed and ran a hand through thick black hair lightly salted with silver. He was thirty-eight years old, six foot two, one hundred and ninety pounds of muscle and sinew. He'd been a cop for twenty years, most of those in Bridgeport, Connecticut, a city with a worse reputation than it deserved, although it had plenty of mean streets all the same. He would still be there if some genius in the governor's office hadn't decided urban police ought to rotate out every once in a while to get a "fresh perspective" and other similar drivel. On the final countdown to retirement, he was eking out his days dodging deer and killing time. Hell of a way to go out.

The phone rang. In the silence of the station house, it sounded like all hell breaking loose. But that would be too much to ask for, wouldn't it?

No, maybe it wouldn't. Three men snatching a fourth. An eyewitness with a partial license plate. Hey, why not? He was still technically on duty, at least for the next twenty minutes. Besides, Mitch Harrison was his relief, and while Mitch seemed like a real nice guy and might someday make a good cop, he was still noticeably wet behind the ears.

Briggs levered himself out of the chair, taking his jacket with him, and headed for the car. He moved without apparent haste but covered the distance swiftly. Within moments he was on the road.

He left the siren off, along with the roof lights. Rookies loved both, but experience showed there were relatively few circumstances when they were useful. While there was little chance the snatch car would still be in the area, he didn't see any reason to advertise his own presence. At the least, he would avoid setting off an uproar at the restaurant.

He parked around the back and killed the engine. A beefy, sandy-haired guy was standing there. He was holding a shotgun.

Briggs sighed. What the hell kind of planet was this, anyway? Hadn't anyone ever told this guy that you did not—repeat, not—stand out in the open holding a gun when you were expecting the cops? He was probably the owner or an employee. He probably had the best of intentions in the world. And he would probably have gotten his head blown off if he'd been anywhere else except "the town that time forgot."

Briggs got out of the car slowly. He had his hand in the inside front of his jacket like he was reaching for a cigarette. In fact, he hadn't smoked in fifteen years. What he was reaching for was his identification. His service revolver was in a holster at the small of his back. If he was wrong about this guy, it was going to seem real far away.

"Put the gun down, sir," he said quietly.

The man looked startled. "What?"

"The gun, put it down." He flashed the small black folder with its gold badge.

The man stared at it, blinked and exhaled sharply. He lowered the gun. "Thank God. Look, I'm afraid we've got a real situation here."

"Okay," Briggs said. That was par for the course as far as he was concerned. "What happened?"

Mike Harrison, as he identified himself, might not be real street smart about cops and guns, but he knew how to report. Must have had some military training, Briggs thought absently as he absorbed what he'd just heard.

"Where's the woman?" he asked.

"Elsabeth? She's inside." Harrison's brow furrowed. "She's real upset. Thinks the guy's in big trouble."

"She may be right," was all Briggs said. He followed Harrison into the kitchen. Most of the staff were trying to work—there were hungry customers waiting. But they kept casting anxious glances at the young woman who sat on a stool at a counter with a large blonde hovering over her.

"Are you sure, honey?" Hermione asked for the twentieth time. "I mean, it was real dark and—"

"I'm sure," Elsabeth said quietly. Her face was pale, her eyes luminously blue. She had chewed on her lower lip, making it slightly swollen. Her thumb had come off.

Briggs blinked, looked again and saw that it was a fake thumb. Somehow that didn't make him feel a whole lot better.

"Miss Grace?" he asked.

She turned her head and met his eyes. Briggs's stomach did a long, leisurely loop-the-loop. Sweet lord, this woman was beautiful. Even pale and frazzled, she just about glowed.

He cleared his throat, pulled up the stool next to her and said quietly, "Tell me what you saw."

He watched her lips as they started to move. Far in the back of his mind, it occurred to him that he had never seen lips quite that soft. Then he stopped thinking about anything other than what she was saying.

"Three men pushed a fourth into a late-model sedan, black, four-door, Connecticut license plate starts with WR9. The three were all large, wearing business suits, aged mid-twenties to early thirties, short hair—one blond, two with darker hair. They looked like they could be football players. The fourth man was smaller, thinner, but the suit he had on was more expensive. He looked to be in his early forties—dark hair, slender face, horn-rimmed glasses. He was also terrified."

"I see," Briggs said slowly. He sat back and looked at her again. She met his gaze steadily. "You're very observant," he said.

She shrugged. "It's part of my job."

"Which is?"

"I'm a magician. Look, it's great to be having this little chat, but don't you think you ought to be trying to find that poor man? His buddies didn't look like they were taking him to a sorority tea party."

A magician? Automatically Briggs ran down the catalog in his mind, the one he'd been keeping just about his whole life. Magician's assistants he'd met— they wore skimpy costumes, stiletto heels, got sawed into pieces, the usual. But no female magicians. There didn't seem to be too many of those.

"It runs in my family," Elsabeth said by way of explanation.

"Okay."

"About the man." She was trying very hard not to show her impatience, but she wasn't having much luck.

"We've got an A.P.B. out based on the preliminary information your boss called in," Briggs said. "I'll add a few more details, but essentially, unless the guy turns up *and* files a complaint, there isn't much for us to go on."

"He was kidnapped," Elsabeth said tensely. "He may not be able to 'turn up,' much less file a complaint."

Which showed that she was at least thinking, Briggs acknowledged. Whoever the guy was, things were definitely not looking good for him. Chances were he'd ticked off some girlfriend's brothers or maybe cheated on a business deal. Unless the state troopers happened to get a sighting—not very likely after dark on winding country roads—he'd probably end up a little sorer and a little wiser.

Or it might be a whole lot more than that. He might wind up dead.

Briggs stood up. "Let's take a drive."

She didn't ask where to, she just followed him out to his car and got in. He noted wryly that when women were that compliant they usually had an ulterior motive. But if that was the case with Elsabeth Grace, she wasn't saying. In fact, she didn't say a word until they'd been driving a good twenty minutes.

Finally she said, "You're not from Redding."

He shook his head. He drove with his left hand on the wheel, an old habit from when he and a partner had been ambushed in the Bronx back when he'd been a New York cop. He hardly ever thought of those days anymore, but the habits formed then had stayed with him.

"Bridgeport," he said. "I'm on . . . liaison with the local police."

"Liaison . . ." She drew the word out as though she liked the way it sounded. Out of the corner of his eye, he saw her smile.

"What did you do?" she asked.

He stiffened. "What do you mean?"

"The way you say it makes it sound like you're being punished, so what did you do?"

He sighed. Sometimes first impressions were right. He'd thought she was smart, and she was. "Put in my papers."

"What does that mean?"

"Filed for retirement. I make twenty years total next month, so I figured it was time to get out. Put in the papers, start the countdown, simple. Then some bozo in the governor's office comes up with this liaison thing. Big-city cops talking to the guys in the boonies." As if they had anything to talk about, which, so far as he could see, they did not.

"So they sent you? Maybe they thought they were doing you a favor."

He made a low, rude noise that told her his response to that. Still, she persisted. "Bridgeport isn't exactly a country club. Maybe somebody just wanted you to take it easy your last few weeks."

That happened to be exactly what Sal D'Angelo, Briggs's lieutenant and friend, had said when he dumped the assignment in his unwilling lap. What he'd also said was, "Life's not all mean streets and cat-sized rats, Briggs. Time you found that out."

Personally he'd take cat-sized rats over elephant-sized deer any day, but try convincing Sal of that. The older man had a romantic's view of nature, probably because he'd never spent much more time in it than Briggs had. Still, Sal liked the idea that there was a simpler, purer world out there somewhere and thought *somebody* ought to give it a look-see.

"So where are we going?" Elsabeth asked.

"To look at some pictures."

She nodded and leaned her head back against the seat. Softly she said, "We'd better hurry."

Chapter 2

Elsabeth closed her eyes for a moment, hoping the brief rest would clear them. She was very tired, her head ached, and her throat was dry, but she wasn't about to give up. They had been at the station house in Bridgeport for more than an hour. She had spent the time leafing through page after page of mug shots, hundreds upon hundreds of faces, all men who had been arrested for at least one significant crime. She knew she shouldn't have been surprised by how many there were; everyone understood that the streets were dangerous and getting more so. But the sheer weight of numbers overwhelmed her. She had rarely felt so depressed.

Beneath that was another equally anxiety-producing sensation. Even as she carefully scrutinized each picture, she was acutely conscious of the man seated near her. Briggs had said little since he'd brought her the books and explained what they were. He simply stayed close, making his way through a pile of paperwork that had accumulated during his stay in what he unabashedly called the "boonies." In the few glances she had stolen, the task looked mind-numbingly dull. But he appeared resigned to it.

He had taken off his jacket, loosened his tie and rolled up his sleeves, the classic actions of a man getting down to work. She surreptitiously admired the broad sweep of his shoulders before she turned yet another page in the book.

Another fifty or so faces and her attention wandered again. He was gathering together a stack of papers. His hands were large, the fingers long and blunt-tipped. His nails were short, clean, but without the gloss of a professional manicure. He would go to a barber shop to get that thick black hair cut, not to a unisex hair salon. He might occasionally indulge in a full-blown shave, complete with hot towels, but she couldn't imagine him getting a facial. He wore his clothes well, but it would have been hard not to, given his large, muscular body which was honed to such graceful elegance. There was nothing artificial or pretentious about him. He was what her great-aunt would have called a man's man, although Georgette admitted she could never understand why they were called that, since such beings were invariably every woman's dream.

Or almost every woman's dream. Elsabeth's own attitude toward the opposite sex had been formed by a painful love affair in college and a few unsatisfying brushes since then. She had decided that she was on the one hand too particular and on the other too vulnerable to allow for the rigors of the modern mating dance. Very simply, she wanted all or nothing—true love, lasting commitment and mutual respect, or a life of independence and dignity unmarred by the failed relationships she had seen so many other people experience. Although there had been times when she was undeniably lonely, she was also convinced she had made the right decision.

At least, she had been convinced.

Briggs looked up, caught her eye and smiled. "You okay?" he asked.

"I guess so. It's just sort of . . . dispiriting."

He had never heard it put that way before, but he understood what she meant. Even though he lived every day of his life close to the sour underbelly of urban existence, he realized there were people like Elsabeth to whom it came as a rude shock. He was sorry she had to lose some of that innocence, but maybe in the long run it would be to the good. Nobody was better off for being naive in this world.

She looked back down at the book. Her index finger traced over one of the pictures. "Most of them are so young."

"I didn't give you the juvies by mistake, did I?" he asked. He took a quick look at the book, confirming that it contained adults only.

"The average age of a felon in this city is about twenty-two," he said matter-of-factly. "You described the perps as being slightly older, so maybe we'll get lucky."

"Maybe," Elsabeth murmured as she returned her attention to the photos. The faces were beginning to run together in her mind. She was afraid they would all start to look alike, but then suddenly...

Her head shot up. "I found one."

She was genuincly astonished. Although she was certain about her description of the men, she had only glimpsed them for a few seconds. Added to that was the sheer number of photographs. It seemed impossible that she would actually be able to match one to a face in the parking lot. Yet she had.

Briggs was on his feet. He came around the table and leaned over her. For a moment she was dizzyingly aware of the faint scent of his after-shave. Nothing very exotic, just straightforward, crisp, masculine—like the man himself.

He whistled softly under his breath and abruptly grinned. He looked exactly like a little boy who had been given an unexpected present.

"Well, I'll be, if it isn't good ol' Dapper Dan Ruglio. I was wondering when he'd turn up again."

"You know him?"

"You might say that. I arrested him a couple of years back on a truck hijacking scam. He should have gone away for four, maybe five years. But he got himself a sharp lawyer and plea-bargained down to six months plus probation. It was a waste."

Something of his frustration and the bitterness that came from it reached Elsabeth. Gently she said, "Surely he won't get off so lightly this time?"

"That depends."

"On what?"

"On the victim. If he turns up alive and refuses to testify, then Ruglio could walk. But on the other hand..."

He didn't finish the thought, but then, he didn't have to. Reminded of exactly what was at stake, Elsabeth redoubled her efforts. Half an hour later she said, "I've got another one."

Briggs stared down at the broad, angry face in the photo. He nodded slowly. "It fits. That's Mick MacMann. He's called Mick the Stick."

"He's not exactly skinny," Elsabeth pointed out.

Briggs hesitated a moment. Quietly he said, "The nickname's because he used a baseball stick to kill a man when he was fifteen years old. He got tried as a juvenile and did three years at some state home. Since then he's been implicated in at least two other killings, all mob-related. He's major bad news."

Elsabeth thought again of the terrified man in the back of the car, and her stomach tightened. "That poor man. I wonder who he could be."

Briggs tapped the book in front of her. "Keep looking," he said grimly. "You may find *him* in there, too."

He left her briefly to amend the A.P.B. with the names of the two identified perps. On his way back he got them both another cup of tea. Elsabeth was once again absorbed in the books. He set the cup at her elbow and settled down again to wait.

An hour later she hit the third one—Charlie "Chumpster" Gingrich, so called for his very large size and very small intellect. Like the first two, he was an enforcer, and—also like them—there were rumors that he'd gone freelance. Everybody was cutting back these days, even the mob. There were plenty of guys out looking for work. These three had apparently found it.

The fourth man, the victim, was the toughest to tap. They had to go to a whole different set of books at a whole different level before Elsabeth got him, too.

"That's the one," she said.

Briggs looked at where her finger was pointing and whistled softly. "Well, well."

Elsabeth sat back in the hard wooden chair. She was exhausted, her head throbbed, and she was filled with the deepest sense of apprehension she had ever known. Part of her wanted to flee and never hear another word about what she had just seen and done. But she'd never run from anything in her life, and she wasn't going to start now.

"Who is he?" she asked.

"Jerome Dickinson. He's an accountant."

"*An accountant?* But . . ."

"Don't let that fool you. Accountants can lead very exciting lives."

Although he answered lightly enough, inside Briggs was seething. Damn, damn and damn. He'd had Dickinson in his jurisdiction, practically under his nose, and he hadn't even known it. For the better part of two decades, Dickinson had managed to stay ahead of the law. He was an inside man, a financial wizard who specialized in making dirty money look clean. Anyone who managed to open him up would have access to a treasure trove of information, enough to put some very serious people away for a very serious amount of time.

And now it looked as though it was too late.

"Maybe he'll still turn up," Briggs said, even though he didn't really think there was a chance. Men like Dickinson, the few there were, got sweet han-

dling from their grateful employers. For that to change
meant that something had gone very wrong in a game
where errors brought only one penalty.

Briggs sighed and ran a hand over his face. "You
need some rest," he told Elsabeth, "and I need to talk
to some people. There's a couch in the captain's office."

"I'd really rather go home."

"We'll get to that." He took her arm and helped her
out of the chair, then led her into the office. The couch
was lumpy, but there was an afghan the captain's wife
had knitted to go with it. Elsabeth didn't need all that
much coaxing to lie down for a little bit.

"Don't go anywhere," Briggs said as he headed for
the door. He needn't have worried. Before he'd even
shut it behind him, Elsabeth was fast asleep.

"I'm telling you," Briggs said, "she's perfect. Near
total recall, calm, articulate, the works. She pegged all
three of them, plus Dickinson, with no hesitation.
She'll be dynamite in court."

Sal took a long puff on his cigar and stared at the
ceiling. He was a big, perpetually rumpled man with
a hangdog expression. Some people, not smart ones,
tended to think he wasn't too bright. It wasn't a mistake anyone made twice. "If we get to court," Sal
said. "If there's actually a case. If she doesn't
get . . . discouraged."

"Yeah," Briggs said quietly.

Sal thought a moment longer. Abruptly he jerked
his feet off the desk, swung them to the floor and
stood up. "Okay, let's see what we can do about finding Dickinson. Meantime, you sit on Miss Grace."

Briggs's eyebrows shot up. "What do you mean, sit?"

"What're you, deaf? Sit means sit. Keep an eye on her, don't let her wander off, don't let her get her pretty head blown to bits." Sal smiled, showing the gold tooth he'd gotten when he was seventeen, long ago in a simpler time. "She is pretty, isn't she?"

Briggs muttered something under his breath and walked out of the office.

Elsabeth was asleep on the couch. Her hair—a shade between brown and red that he couldn't put a name to but which looked fantastic—was spread out over the broken-down cushion. Part of it obscured her face, not enough, though, to leave any doubt about exactly how pretty she was. She was lying half on her side so that the curve of one hip was clearly visible, along with the deep indentation of her waist. Her breasts swelled gently against the pleated shirtfront.

She looked gorgeous, ripe, unspoiled, exquisite. Also vulnerable.

Briggs sighed. He seemed to have been doing that a lot in the last few hours. He sat down in a chair near the couch and waited for her to wake up. It didn't take long. He half expected her to be mad at finding him looking at her, but if she was, she didn't show it. She just blinked once, then again, almost like a cat waking up, and looked at him calmly.

"What's wrong?" she asked.

"Nothing," he lied.

He took her downstairs to the cafeteria that was open twenty-four hours a day and bought her a cup of tea. It was even worse than the stuff from the office pot, and she grimaced when she tasted it, but she didn't say anything. He found himself wondering if she was always this quiet.

"You don't talk much, do you?" he said.

She shrugged. "Depends. I can do a pretty good line of patter when I need to."

He frowned. She sounded like a con man, which had to be a double contradiction because A, she was the least dishonest person he could remember meeting, and B, she was also the most feminine.

She smiled at his discomfort. "Do you know much about magicians?"

"Not really. I've seen a few on TV."

"If you think about it, you'll realize that magicians always talk a lot. It's a form of distraction. For instance, we might talk about how hard the trick we're doing really is, and how we're not sure it will work because in the last hundred years it's only worked maybe two or three times, and even then no one was sure why. While we're doing all this talking, we'll be working with a few props like this cup of tea maybe, moving it back and forth, asking you to look at it really carefully, calling your attention to this napkin—" She fluttered it in front of his eyes. "But none of that really means anything when we—" She reached over and removed a large purple flower from behind his left ear.

"Pretty," she said with a smile.

Briggs frowned again. She was making him nervous. "You had it up your sleeve," he said, looking at the closely tailored sleeve of her jacket and wondering exactly how she could have got the huge flower up there.

"Maybe, or maybe you just like to go around with flowers behind your ears." She reached over again and pulled out an orange one, followed by a blue one, a red one and finally a multicolored one.

"Of course," she said, smiling broadly now, "I can understand how this sort of thing could get embarrassing for a policeman, so why don't we just get rid of the evidence?"

The flowers disappeared. One second they were there, and the next they weren't. He was looking right at her—and them. He didn't so much as blink. She was holding five large paper flowers on thin wire stems; then she wasn't.

"How did you—" he began, knowing that he was looking like an idiot but unable to do much about it.

She stood up, took a little bow to acknowledge the applause of the half dozen night people watching from nearby tables, and said, "I can't tell."

Then she sat down again and finished her tea. He had just asked her if she wanted another cup and she had declined when he saw Sal standing at the door.

"Wait here," he told Elsabeth.

Sal didn't waste any time. In a low voice made rough by fatigue, he said, "Dickinson turned up faster than I thought he would."

The tone said everything. If the accountant had still been alive, Sal would have been excited, very up, not tired and frustrated.

Briggs made a sound deep in his throat. He didn't even know he did it. Automatically his gaze switched back to Elsabeth sitting at the table. She was looking into the empty teacup as if she could see something there.

"Get her out of here," Sal said. "Tomorrow—
make that this afternoon—she'll talk to the D.A. Then
we'll decide where to go from there."

Briggs shot past frowning and hit full-force scowl.
Certain criminal types—muggers of little old ladies,
smut peddlers, drug dealers—had been known to
shrivel up before such a look. Sal himself was hardly
immune. He held up a beefy hand to deflect it. "I
know, I know, the whole thing stinks. Just do the best
you can."

"What about a hotel?" Briggs demanded. "Someplace she can't be immediately traced?"

Sal glanced over at Briggs's table, where Elsabeth
sat with her russet hair falling over her back and her
body snugly outlined by the magician's suit. He
grinned. "You want to take the lady to a hotel, it's fine
with me." He turned and left, vanishing through the
cafeteria's swinging doors with the firm walk of a man
who had successfully unloaded a problem on somebody he was sure could handle it.

Briggs didn't share his confidence. Warily he went
back to Elsabeth. Without sitting down, he said,
"Dickinson's dead."

For a moment she didn't respond at all. Only slowly
did she lift her head and look at him. "I'm sorry."

She meant it. He could see the pain and regret
working at her. Gently he laid his hand on her shoulder, instantly aware of how delicate her bones felt.

"Don't," he said. "There's nothing you could have
done."

Her eyes were bleak. "Picked them out quicker."

"And then what? We still would have to find them
before they got rid of him. That kind of stuff only

happens on television. Anyway, we stand a better than fair chance of getting convictions.'' He hesitated. ''That is, as long as you're willing to testify.''

Almost twenty years as a cop, dedicating himself to bringing some shadow of justice to the chaos all around him, and he still couldn't resist the niggling little hope that she'd say no.

''Of course, I will,'' was what she actually said.

''Great.'' He forced himself to sound enthusiastic, although he could tell it wasn't working. Elsabeth shot him a puzzled look.

''Is there something about all this that I'm missing?'' she asked.

No, Briggs thought, only about a million things. But the cafeteria wasn't the place to get into any of them.

''Let's just say that some people aren't going to be too happy about this,'' he said as he stood aside to indicate they were leaving. ''So until we've got the perps under wraps, we'll need to keep an eye on you.''

That seemed clear enough to him, but it wasn't to Elsabeth. She ignored the flare of apprehension that went through her and stood up. ''What do you mean, 'keep an eye' on me?''

''It's no big deal,'' he said, taking her arm. ''We're just going to put you someplace where nobody'll bother you. There's a hotel we use for this kind of thing....''

She stopped dead in her tracks and stared at him. ''A hotel? I'm not going to any hotel. I'm going home.''

''That's not a good idea. There's a chance they could find out who you are and where you live. A hotel is much better. There's a very nice place we use not too far from here—"

"No."

"Look," he said, "I know this isn't what you bargained for, but it really is for the best. These guys are nobody to mess with."

"I don't care who they are. I'm going home." Gently but firmly she disengaged the arm he was holding. "Thank you for your help, Detective Caldwell. Please let me know if there's any progress on the case."

Without a backward glance she walked away.

Briggs was not normally slow on the uptake. On the contrary, only lightning-fast reflexes had kept him alive in Vietnam and a few times since. But she took him by surprise. Elsabeth had reached the cafeteria door before he responded. He crossed the distance between them in long, firm strides and stepped right in front of her, blocking her way. His big, hard body and the unrelenting gleam in his steel-gray eyes made it clear he wasn't going to stand for any more nonsense.

"You're not leaving here by yourself."

"I don't think you can actually detain me," she said softly.

"Think again." His voice lowered to a rough-edged growl. "You're a material witness, Ms. Grace. You can be placed in protective custody."

A shadow of uncertainty flickered across features that he had come to realize were as calm as they were beautiful. Or perhaps that was a part of their beauty. He wasn't sure, and this wasn't the time to figure it out.

"You'd actually put me in jail?" she asked, incredulous at the mere thought, but no longer dismissing it.

He hesitated. Theoretically, under extreme circumstances, that could be done. But he would have the devil's own time convincing any district attorney, much less a judge, to go along with that idea.

"No," he said finally, "we wouldn't."

"But you were willing to threaten it?"

He met her eyes without apology. "It is true that you could be in danger. You should not be by yourself."

She thought a moment. The face looming above her was hard and implacable, but not lacking in sensitivity. He was a strong man and a forceful one, but he was also honest. He could have lied to her about the danger and about going to jail.

Abruptly she remembered the face of the man in the back of the car. Jerome Dickinson had been terrified, and with hindsight she knew why. He had realized that he was going to die.

She had no such knowledge, but she was afraid, that was for certain. Vaguely she resented Briggs for bringing the fear home to her even as she knew she should be grateful to him.

"All right," she said. Quickly she added, "But not a hotel. I really will be much safer at home. When you see it, I think you'll understand why."

Briggs doubted that, but he realized he'd gotten the best deal he could. Reluctantly he agreed.

Chapter 3

The house stood at the end of a quarter mile-long dirt lane that had only one outlet. It was surrounded by shoulder-high hedges and a scattering of old, gnarled trees. In the darkness it looked small, unprepossessing and vulnerable.

"I don't see why you thought you'd be safer here," Briggs said as he got out of the car. Personally he didn't like the feel of it at all. It was too quiet, too solitary. Anybody could be sneaking around in the woods nearby planning anything at all. Instinctively his fingers curled, seeking the cool, steel touch of his gun.

"You need daylight to really appreciate it," Elsabeth said. She had driven in ahead of him. They had stopped by the Red Rooster to pick up her car, Briggs not wanting to leave it there overnight where it might attract attention. Once he saw it, he changed that might to definitely would have. He'd never seen so old and decrepit a vehicle. He would, in fact, have bet money that it couldn't possibly stay on the road. But he'd been wrong, even though it was still sputtering and shuddering after the ignition was turned off. He wondered absently if cars could be possessed and decided that if this one was, he didn't want to meet whatever had taken up residence in it.

Elsabeth walked up the flagstone path and put the key in the lock. "There used to be a rock quarry here. This house is built almost on the edge of it. The way we came in is fine, but the other three sides are precipices." She smiled puckishly. "You wander strictly at your own peril."

Briggs was impressed despite himself, but he didn't have much time to think about that. The moment the door swung open, a high-pitched beeping noise shattered the quiet.

"What the hell—" he began.

"It's the alarm system," Elsabeth said. Deftly she punched in a numbered code, and the beeping stopped. "You must see a lot of these."

True enough, but he hadn't expected one in so remote a house. "Did you install it?" he asked.

Elsabeth shook her head. She had left the hall light on when she went to work. By its glow she looked very young and more than a little tired.

"My great-aunt Georgette put it in. I inherited the house from her."

Briggs stepped into the entry hall, glancing around at the wood-paneled walls and slate floor. The stones sloped slightly toward their centers, as though they had been walked on for a very long time.

"Did she have some kind of trouble here?" Briggs asked.

Elsabeth shook her head. "She did a favor for someone who happened to run a security business. He insisted on giving her one, and she didn't have the heart to turn him down."

"Are you always conscientious about using it?"

"I try," she said. "Not all the shows I do are small, close-up stuff like at the restaurant. I have some fairly expensive equipment that I wouldn't want to lose."

That made sense. It also made his job easier. He was beginning to think that not going to the hotel had been the right decision after all.

"I don't know about you," Elsabeth said, "but I'm starved. How about we eat?"

"Sounds good," Briggs said. In fact, he was ravenous, not having eaten since lunch. He needed no encouragement to follow her along the hall to the kitchen. It ran the entire width of the house in the back and was reached down a short flight of steps. The floor was soft gray stone, like the entry hall. Dark beams crisscrossed the ceiling. The walls were white, except where they had been covered with blue-and-white delft tiles. The cabinets were old but solid, made of oak, he thought. A state-of-the-art gas stove with six burners held pride of place along one wall. The opposite wall boasted an enormous refrigerator. Bunches of drying herbs hung from wrought-iron hooks. There were a few woven rugs on the floor and a pitcher of fresh flowers on the battered wooden table. Everything spoke of comfort, ease and long, affectionate use.

"Nice," Briggs murmured. He thought of his own sterile, virtually unused kitchen and winced inwardly. His ex-wife, Patricia, had never liked to cook. They'd eaten out most of the time, or microwaved. On his own he was hopeless. But he could remember the smells from his mother's kitchen. It hadn't been anywhere near as big or fancy as this one, but somehow they both felt the same.

"Georgette loved to cook," Elsabeth said. She gestured to a row of stools next to the counter. "Sit down. I'll fix you a drink."

"Club soda, if you have it."

She nodded and began taking things out of the refrigerator. He watched, struck by how smooth and economical her movements were. She felt him watching and glanced up uncertainly.

"I'm sorry," he said. "I'm just not..." He trailed off, not knowing what to say to her. How could he explain that a beautiful, pleasant, courageous woman was not the sort of person he encountered every day? That, in fact, he couldn't remember the last time he had seen such a creature, much less actually sat in the same room with her while she fixed him a meal.

Not that he'd been exactly celibate since the divorce. There had been a few women—very few, now that he thought about it—whose company he had enjoyed both in and out of bed. But none of them had captured his full attention the way Elsabeth did.

"How long have you been a magician?" he asked, partly because he was curious, but mostly to fill up the silence between them.

"I'm not sure." She thought it over as she tore lettuce into a bowl. "I started so young that I can't remember a time when I wasn't doing magic. But I didn't turn professional until I was in high school.''

''Waited that long, did you?''

She laughed. ''Actually, most families like mine put the kids on stage early, if only to help them get experience. I know people who were performing before they could walk.''

He took another sip of the club soda and watched her slice several tomatoes with a speed that made him worry about her fingertips. ''So why didn't yours?''

She put the tomatoes into the bowl along with the lettuce and began mixing soft-green olive oil with a plum-hued vinegar. ''There's been a split in my family ever since Grandfather Malcolm decided to become a lawyer instead of a magician.''

Briggs widened his eyes in mock horror. ''A lawyer? What could he have been thinking of?''

''Nobody knows for sure,'' Elsabeth said seriously. ''But it may have had something to do with what happened to him when he was a baby. You see, his mother was Adana of the Nile. Her father, my great-great-grandfather, was Max the Magnificent, the creator of the Indian Sands Trick.'' She paused to see if he understood the significance of all this.

When it became clear that he didn't, she said, ''Anyway, the family was very big in magic. Adana married Daniel 'Daredevil' Dawes. They toured worldwide to enormous acclaim. Malcolm was born while they were in Europe. One day his nursemaid goofed and set him down in a trunk that was actually a prop for one of Adana and Danny's tricks. Malcolm disappeared—went 'poof,' as we say in the business—setting off the usual hue and cry. He turned up in the sixth row of the theater sucking on a corner of his blanket and seemed no worse for the experience. But he never showed the slightest interest in magic and insisted on going to law school instead."

"Shocking," Briggs said. He took another sip of his drink to confirm that it was indeed club soda. He was beginning to feel a little woozy, as if the real world were slipping gently but inexorably out of focus.

"Malcolm was your grandfather?" he asked, thinking that if he could just get it sorted out, he would be okay.

Elsabeth nodded. She set the salad on the table and turned her attention to the lamb chops she had slipped under the broiler. While she was at it, she put a loaf of French bread in the oven to crisp.

"Malcolm's son was my father, Philip. He started out very straight, just the way Malcolm wanted. But during his junior year at Princeton, a magic show happened to pass through town. That was it for Philip. Some people run off with the circus, he ran off with the magic show. He must have had innate talent, because he picked things up very quickly. He also met my mother, Marjorie, who was ushering at one of the theaters where he performed. They eloped, and about a year later, I was born."

"Where are your parents now?"

"Dead," Elsabeth said quietly. "They were killed in a train wreck in Iowa twenty years ago. Grandfather Malcolm took me to live with him in Boston, but I wasn't very happy there. Great-aunt Georgette, his sister, convinced him to let me spend time with her." She smiled at the memory. "Georgette had stayed in the business. She performed professionally until she was seventy years old. She taught me everything I know.''

"And she left you this house?"

Elsabeth nodded. The lamb chops were done. She set them on a warmed platter garnished with slivers of fresh rosemary and deftly sliced bread. "We eat."

He supposed that, as such things went, it was a simple meal. But it was also startlingly delicious. The flavors seemed to melt in his mouth, the textures merging and complementing each other. He couldn't remember when he had last been fed with such care or success.

"You're a good cook," he said as he looked at her across the plain wooden table set with blue-and-white woven place mats and china that matched.

"Georgette insisted on it. She said a person who couldn't cook was essentially useless."

He grimaced. "She wouldn't have made much of me, then."

"Oh, I don't know about that," Elsabeth said. "Georgette was very forgiving of men."

Which sounded like a promising line of conversation, but one Elsabeth was not inclined to pursue. Instead she deftly changed the subject.

"Why did you go into police work?"

He leaned back in his chair, stretching his long legs out, and smiled faintly. "The pay's good, so are the benefits, and the hours aren't bad."

"I'm serious."

"So am I. You don't think that's enough reason to join the force?"

"No," Elsabeth said, "I don't. But it is your business, and if you don't want to talk about it . . ."

He sighed. She'd brought him into her home, cooked for him, told him all about herself. Under the circumstances, it wouldn't kill him to open up a little.

"I was in Vietnam," he said. "A lot of what I saw there, I didn't like. I came home with an idea about making the world better. The police force seemed as good a way as any."

"Were you always in Bridgeport?"

He shook his head. "I was born and raised in Brooklyn, so it was natural to join up in New York. I spent ten years there before I came out here."

"You said you were retiring soon?"

"That's right. Twenty years is enough for me. Besides, I've got some ideas about other things I want to do."

Actually there was really only one "thing." Five years ago, Briggs had finally gotten down to doing what he'd always just dreamed about doing—writing. He'd worked nights, weekends, any odd hour he could manage on a battered old manual typewriter he'd bought because it looked like something a real writer would have. The first stages had been grueling; he'd been so disgusted with his output that he'd almost quit. But then it had all started to come together. Not in any great flash, and it had never gotten easy. But it had gotten good.

Good enough that he'd published his first book the year before, a police thriller the critics called "riveting" and "terrifyingly real." The book hadn't been a bestseller, but it had sold well enough to land him a substantial contract. He still had the old typewriter, but he'd also acquired a whiz-bang computer that he had to admit made his life a whole lot easier. He'd reached the point where he was ready to turn in his shield and start writing full-time.

But first he had to get through the next few weeks *and* get Elsabeth Grace safely to court.

"Let me help you," he said as she stood to clear the table. They worked together in companionable silence. But when it was done, the awkwardness settled over them again.

Softly, not looking at him, Elsabeth said, "I'll fix up the guest room."

"You don't have to bother," he said quickly. "If you'll just give me whatever's needed, I'll take care of it."

They went together into the little hallway where the downstairs linen closet was located. He held out both his arms, and she heaped them with sheets, blankets and towels.

"It still gets cold here at night," she said, explaining the blankets.

"I've noticed."

"But the heating system is pretty good. I don't think you'll be uncomfortable. If you are, there's a thermostat in the living room."

"It's all right," he reassured her gently. "I'll be fine."

Still she hesitated. In the dim light of the hallway, they stood close together. He could smell the flowery perfume of her hair and feel the warmth of her skin. His mouth was suddenly dry.

"Thank you," she said softly.

His brows drew together in a hard, black line. "What for?"

"For coming here, for keeping me safe."

Oh, that. The most desirable woman he'd ever met, and wasn't it nice how *safe* she felt with him?

"It's my job," he said.

She gave him a small, uncertain smile. "Good night."

When she was gone, he went into the guest room, where he made up the bed with vicious speed. He dumped the towels in the adjoining bath, along with the shaving kit he'd grabbed from his desk earlier. Stripped to his briefs, he lay down on the bed with his arms folded behind his head and stared up at the ceiling. He told himself there was no point in trying to sleep.

Two minutes later he was doing exactly that.

Briggs woke to sunlight and a crushing weight on his chest. He opened his eyes a slit and found himself staring directly into a pair of unblinking topaz marbles. They were attached to a large, gray-furred body that had settled directly on top of him.

"I think I should tell you," he said, his voice roughened by sleep, "that I don't like cats."

The cat continued to stare at him for a moment longer before stretching out a paw. Slowly, with unhurried grace, it began to wash.

"Great," Briggs muttered. He sat up abruptly, spilling the cat onto the bed. It shot him a knife-edged glare, turned and vanished through the partly opened door.

Briggs followed not long after. He had paused only long enough to pull on his clothes, brush his teeth and splash cold water on his face. Anything more could wait until he'd had a chance to assess the situation.

Falling asleep last night had been bad enough, but to sleep deeply and without dreams as he had was unforgivable. He couldn't imagine what had gotten into him. Normally, even at the best of times, he slept lightly and woke frequently. But not last night. Last night he could have been a child again, so innocently had he slept.

Elsabeth was in the kitchen. She was wearing a cotton T-shirt with matching overalls in a soft mauve shade that complemented the russet highlights of her hair. The cat was poised on the counter next to her. She was mixing something in a yellow pottery bowl and humming.

"Oh," she said when she looked up and saw him, "there you are. How did you sleep?"

"Like the dead. It must be this country air." He tried to make light of it, but that was hard to do. Last night, in the magician's rig, she had been beautiful. But now, fresh-faced and rested, she was magical herself.

"Coffee?" he inquired, thinking that a good stiff jolt would help restore him to sanity.

She poured him a mugful. It was strong, no-nonsense coffee, with a hint of something he couldn't quite place.

"Cardamom," she explained. "I hope you don't mind. I used to drink coffee with sugar, then I tried artificial sweeteners, but I didn't really like them. A little ground cardamom gets rid of the harsh edge."

"Perfect," Briggs murmured, thinking that he'd never had a better cup of coffee, or a better night's rest, or a better reason to hightail it out of there as fast as he possibly could. A man could get very comfortable with Elsabeth Grace. He could get very used to all that beauty and gentleness, great food and fantastic coffee to boot. He could start thinking that life didn't get much better.

But not Briggs Caldwell. He was a loner, and besides, he had other plans.

"I need to check in," he said abruptly.

"There's a phone in the den." There was also one in the kitchen, but she had, typically, thought of his possible need for privacy.

As he turned away she said, "Are omelets all right for breakfast?"

"Yeah, sure, anything." He beat a hasty retreat and spent longer on the phone than he really needed to. What he learned did nothing to improve his mood.

He came back to find the table set with fluffy omelets oozing cheese and herbs, crisp toast, crockery jars of preserves, fresh-squeezed orange juice and more of the fantastic coffee.

"This is really more than I usually eat," he said.

Elsabeth smiled. "Just have whatever you like."

He sat down across the table from her and tried to look stern. But the first mouthful of the omelet undid him. She really was a terrific cook.

"You don't have to go to so much trouble," he said more softly.

"It's no trouble at all," Elsabeth replied.

The cat walked across the kitchen. It turned its head and blinked at Briggs. Tail high, stalking invisible prey, it drifted away.

Deciding that he couldn't put it off much longer, Briggs said, "Somebody called the Red Rooster last night. They said they'd heard a disturbance and wondered if anyone else had noticed anything. Fortunately your boss, Mike, had his wits about him. He said if they wanted any information, they could call the police.''

Elsabeth put her fork down slowly. ''You think someone was trying to find out who saw the men abduct Dickinson?''

Briggs nodded. ''You did yell at them. They know they were seen, and they know it was by a woman. Now they've got to narrow the field.'' He paused a moment before he asked, ''How well do you know the people at the Inn?''

Elsabeth looked taken aback. ''You mean Mike and the others? I don't know. . . . Pretty well, I guess. I've worked there for about four months now. They all seem like nice people.''

''They're going to get a chance to prove it,'' Briggs said dryly.

''I don't understand. . . .''

He put his elbows on the table, leaned across and looked at her hard. ''Somebody is going to try to get them to talk. Dickinson was a wealthy man in his own right from the work he did, but he shuffled money for men who could buy and sell him a thousand times over. When they want information, they don't hesitate to get it.''

Elsabeth's eyes were very wide, as inscrutable as the cat's. But whatever she was thinking, she wasn't saying. Maybe she thought she could just snap her fingers and make it all go ''poof.''

''The D.A. wants to see you this morning,'' Briggs said. It was better for her to confront the reality of it head-on. That, more than anything else, would keep her alive.

She nodded but said nothing. For the half hour or so it took them to straighten up and get ready to go, she remained silent. Briggs guessed that she was lost in her thoughts. He would have liked to know what they were, but he figured he'd already pushed her hard enough.

Besides, there would be time for that later. He'd see to it.

Chapter 4

After they arrived at police headquarters, Briggs stashed Elsabeth in a second-floor conference room and went off to do various things she understood to involve "Ummph-ummp" and "hrumph-uhm."

Okay, so he wasn't the most articulate man she had ever come across. But he was the handsomest, toughest, sexiest, most fascinating... her thoughts went on in that general vein until she thought her head would go merrily spinning into space where it would undoubtedly have been a good deal more at home. Due mostly to the fact that she hadn't slept very well the night before. Or at all.

She was cooking, which anyone who actually knew her could have told Briggs was a bad sign. It meant she was turning—as Georgette had always put it—broody. Not that Elsabeth had ever gone broody over a man before. She hadn't, which was a major part of the problem in itself.

Usually she cooked when she was trying to work out a new magic trick. The simple, pleasing action of putting food together soothed her in a way she couldn't explain. It freed her mind to wander down the strange byways that led to acts of fabled legerdemain.

She hadn't told Briggs—because there was no way to do so without sounding awfully taken with herself—but she happened to be fairly big in the world of magic. Had she chosen to, she could have had a career touring the major capitals, doing television specials, even—be still, my beating heart—playing Vegas. But she had tried it before Georgette died and stayed with it long enough to know that such a life wasn't for her. Now she made the bulk of her living coming up with new acts, which she sold to other magicians. She had rapidly become known as an innovator and teacher. The act she did at the Red Rooster and a few other similar places was just a way of staying limber.

She glanced at the clock on the stark white wall. Briggs was taking his time. Not that she could blame him. There were probably lots of things to do that she couldn't even imagine. But that left her with the problem of what to do with herself.

Not that she was really at loose ends. One of the many good things about being a magician was that no matter how skilled you became, you could never afford to rest on your laurels. Practice, practice, practice, Georgette had always said, drilling it into Elsabeth until she could no more think of going through a day without magic than she could without breathing.

She settled more comfortably in the chair and took a deck of cards out of the copious pocket of her overalls. She shuffled rapidly, then spread the cards out face-down on the table in front of her. Quickly she picked out the three of hearts, the two of spades, and the seven of clubs, put the cards back in the deck and shuffled again. Over and over she repeated the exercise—shuffling, spreading, selecting exactly the same cards. In a performance, she would be talking at the same time, directing the audience's attention to some trivial portion of the activity such as the cuts that really only returned the cards to their designated location.

As she worked, the little couplet Georgette had taught her drifted through her mind: Eight kings threatened to save/Nine fair ladies for one sick knave.

The seemingly meaningless rhyme was actually a memory device for turning an ordinary, unmarked pack of playing cards into a prearranged pack. Using such a pack, a magician could produce any card apparently at will, no matter how many times an audience thought the pack had been cut or shuffled. The prearranged pack was a staple tool, almost as basic as the thumb tip. But Elsabeth never tired of working with it. The possibilities were endless even as the routine was relaxing.

She was still working with the cards when the sound of raised voices in the hallway interrupted her concentration. Frowning, she put the cards back in her pocket. She could make out Briggs's voice and that of another man, but they were far away and there was too much other noise to make out what they were saying.

At any rate, she didn't have to wonder for long. The voices broke off, replaced by firm, angry footsteps. A moment later the conference room door banged open.

Briggs stepped in, scowling. He looked tired, rumpled and grim. That last part pulled at Elsabeth's heart. She hated to think that she was the cause of such concern.

A tall, slender man stepped into the room with Briggs. He had dark blond, blow-dried hair and wore a meticulously tailored suit. As if to offset Briggs's dourness, he smiled broadly, dropped his briefcase into the chair, and held out his hand.

"Hi, there, I'm Dexter Leary, the Assistant District Attorney. It's great to meet you, Miss Grace, and may I say how very much we all appreciate what you're doing. It's a shame more people aren't as public-spirited."

Briggs made a rude sound deep in his throat. "Cut the baloney, Leary. If you want to show the witness your appreciation, try giving her some actual protection."

The prosecutor continued to smile, but the effort was strained and did not reach his eyes. "Detective Caldwell isn't giving himself enough credit, Miss Grace. We feel that you couldn't be in better hands."

Never mind that at the moment those hands looked as though they wanted to wrap themselves around the lawyer's throat.

Leary sat down in an adjoining chair, taking care to lift his trousers so as to preserve their razor-sharp crease. He let the smile go and put on his serious look.

This consisted of widening his brown eyes slightly and gazing directly at Elsabeth.

"I'm going to be frank with you, Miss Grace. This department—like every other justice department in the country—is operating under some pretty serious budgetary constraints. We just don't have the manpower we'd like to have. But, and I stress this, that doesn't mean for a moment that you won't be getting our absolute best efforts."

"That'll be a real consolation to the survivors," Briggs growled.

Leary waved a hand, dismissing his concern.

Leary's casual dismissal was enough reason for Elsabeth to consider it seriously. The previous night she'd wanted only to get back to her own home where she knew she would feel safe. She hadn't considered that if anyone did try to get at her, Briggs would bear the brunt of the attack. It was at least as likely that he would be hurt as it was that she would be. Perhaps even more than hurt.

That was enough to send a stab of dread through her. Quickly she said, "I think I may have been too hasty, Mr. Leary, when I insisted on going home last night. If Detective Caldwell is going to be solely responsible for my safety, he should be the one to decide where I stay."

Leary blinked nervously and attempted another smile. "Yes, well, actually you were on the right track, Miss Grace. We have no reason to think that the perpetrators have any idea who you are, and from what I understand, your house is in a fairly secure location to begin with."

"I didn't say that," Briggs interrupted. "I said it could be worse." He was silently condemning himself for making even that much of an admission. Typically, Leary had seized on it as an excuse to pinch pennies even further. This wasn't the first time he and the D.A.'s office had gone head-to-head on issues related to money. Leary had aspirations far beyond his present position and he thought guarding the taxpayer's money as though it was his own was the way to get there. That wasn't such a bad idea to start with but Leary carried it to ridiculous extremes. It was one of the reasons Briggs was getting out.

"A hotel would create a whole set of problems in and of itself," Leary was saying. "All in all, the present setup is probably the best. Besides," he added magnanimously, "we don't want to interfere too much in the normal course of your life."

As if being the sole witness in a mob murder case hadn't already done that.

With skill Elsabeth couldn't help but admire, Leary changed the subject. He drew her attention back to the suspects, having her identify them yet again and explain exactly what she had seen. When she was finally done, he nodded decisively.

"You'll be very impressive in court, Miss Grace, and you'll never regret this. Not many of us get the chance to make a real difference."

"How do you know what she'll regret?" Briggs demanded. He'd had about all he could take of Leary. The man would sell his own grandmother for a high-profile conviction.

Sensing that the hostility between the two was about to explode, Elsabeth intervened. "About going to

court, Mr. Leary, does that mean you're confident
you'll be able to find these men and arrest them?''

"Absolutely," he said. "It's only a matter of time."

He picked up his briefcase, got to his feet, and trot-
ted toward the door. With a parting smile, he said,
"Don't worry about a thing. This will be wrapped up
before you know it."

In the silence that followed his departure, Elsabeth
stared down at the table. She could feel the anger
coming off Briggs in waves. It frightened her, but at
the same time made her feel strangely secure. He was
enraged at Leary but he wasn't about to let that get the
better of him.

Slowly but implacably, Briggs forced himself to
calm down. "You've just seen a shining example of
the judicial system in progress," he said expression-
lessly. "I'm sure you'll sleep better at night just
knowing you're in such good hands."

Elsabeth stood up. She shoved both her fists into the
pockets of her overalls so he wouldn't see them trem-
bling. Head high, eyes level, she said, "If I were in
Leary's hands, I really would be worried. But I'm not,
thank God. Now can we please get out of here?"

Briggs was only too happy to agree. "I've got to
pick up some stuff at my place," he said as they left
the parking lot. "But that won't take long."

Elsabeth nodded. She felt better just being outside
again, in the sunshine with Briggs. Besides, she was
curious to see where a street-smart cop with an aversion to nature lived.

The answer surprised her. Briggs wasn't too happy
about the "boonies" but he seemed happy enough
with wide-open spaces. Certainly that description fit

the view from his waterfront condo. The day was clear enough for her to see all the way to Long Island, lying flat and green on the horizon. In between was the water, dotted with tiny whitecaps and the usual assortment of boats.

The apartment itself was a revelation. Part of a complex built in the mid-eighties during the great Fairfield County real estate boom, it had undoubtedly been intended to bring much more than its eventual selling price. The rooms were spacious and well-designed. Huge, unobstructed windows let in the spectacular view.

"Make yourself at home," Briggs said as he disappeared into what she supposed was the bedroom. Taking him at his word, she got a can of soda out of the fridge, one of the few items in it, and wandered around the living room.

The furniture was spare but comfortable looking, the colors mainly sand with touches of aquamarine and mauve. The effect was vaguely southwestern, but with a strong sense of sea meeting land. Beyond the living room was a patio and to the other side of that was the second bedroom. Elsabeth's eyes rounded as she stood in the doorway, taking it in.

The room was lined with books. From floor to ceiling, they covered every available wall. In the center of the room stood a desk that seemed submerged in papers, notepads and more books. Beside the desk was a smaller table holding what appeared to be a state-of-the-art computer system.

Maybe he conducted some of his investigations from his home? She imagined him linking into some super-powerful police computer, using it to track down criminals in relentless pursuit of justice day or night…

One of the books on a nearby shelf caught her eye. It looked familiar. She had seen it in bookstores not too long ago. Somebody had recommended it to her but she'd been so busy she hadn't had a chance to read it. Now she took a closer look. The name on the spine was Caldwell. There was a picture of Briggs on the inside back cover.

So Briggs Caldwell was a writer. If his desk was anything to go by, he was hard at work on a new book. No wonder he was looking forward to "retirement."

He was waiting for her in the hall when she re-emerged. Unabashedly she said, "I took your advice."

The sight of her in the privacy of his own home reminded Briggs of how attracted he was to her. It sounded like such a cliché but she lit up the place like no woman he had ever known. There was something warm and real about Elsabeth that he responded to at the deepest level of his being.

"What advice?" he asked distractedly. The problem with being so attracted to her was that it wreaked havoc with his concentration. Just when he needed all his faculties to keep her alive, he couldn't follow a simple conversation. Great.

"To make myself at home," she said. "You're a writer."

He blushed. It was both unexpected and charming. "Not exactly. I wrote one book that happened to get published."

"Which puts you one ahead of most of the rest of the world."

Briggs shrugged. He was obscurely pleased that she'd found out about his book but it also put him on the spot. Next thing she'd be wanting to read it, which he really hoped she wouldn't. There was a fair amount of himself in the main character. That had bothered him at first, but finally he'd accepted it. At least until now. Now he knew that before she got a head start on learning about him, he wanted to have a better handle on what made her tick. It seemed only fair.

"I'm all set," he said, hefting the small bag he held. "Let's go."

He probably set some kind of record driving back to Redding. Once there, they stopped at the station long enough for him to check in and make a few arrangements of his own. He had no trouble lining up additional patrols of the road where Elsabeth lived. The police would do a drive-by every hour, more if they could possibly manage it. Satisfied that he was getting at least some cooperation, Briggs drove Elsabeth home.

After extracting her promise to stay in the house with the alarm system on, he decided to grab a quick shower.

Except that there wasn't one, quick or otherwise. The guest bathroom held a pedestal sink, commode and huge claw-footed tub. No shower.

He sighed, turned on the taps and dropped the little rubber stopper into place. While the tub was filling, he shaved quickly. Then he stripped off the rest of his clothes and stepped into the tub.

He was pleasantly surprised to discover that he could stretch out full-length with only his head propped on one edge. The tub was so large that his feet

barely touched the opposite end. He put his head back
and closed his eyes, smiling. This was more like it. No
wonder showers had taken a while to catch on.

He soaked for ten minutes, all he would allow himself, before climbing out and drying off with the large,
fluffy bath towels Elsabeth had provided. They
smelled faintly of lavender. Ordinarily he would have
presumed that came from a laundry softener. But he'd
noticed the bunches of flowers drying in the kitchen
and suspected it was the real thing.

Just like Elsabeth. He wiped the mist from the mirror and scowled at his reflection. Silently he reminded himself of who and what he was. This would
not be a good time to forget.

When he came back into the kitchen, she was
standing at the enormous stove stirring a pot of soup.
Her hips were thrust slightly to one side with her
weight on one foot. She looked lost in thought.

He cleared his throat. "That smells good. What is
it?"

"Oh, you're done—" She took in the gleaming
black hair, smooth-shaven face, crisp shirt open at the
collar, and fresh khaki pants. He looked utterly masculine and very much in charge.

"I think I left some hot water," he said, "But not
much. It's been a long time since I saw a tub like that."

"It's great, isn't it?" She was glad to seize on so in-
nocuous a subject until the image of him stretched out
naked in the tub popped unbidden into her mind.
Abruptly she blushed.

"The soup is red pepper," she said, hoping he'd
think the color in her cheeks came from standing over

a hot stove. "I'll chill it for dinner and we can have it with some cold chicken, if that's all right."

"It's fine, but you really don't have to bother."

"It's no trouble. I usually have something light to eat before I go to work."

"Speaking of which…we need to talk about that."

She frowned, hoping he wasn't going to create a problem. "I have a standing commitment at the Red Rooster. I don't much like the idea of letting them down."

"I thought you'd take the opposite view. After what happened, some people would never have wanted to see the place again."

Elsabeth shrugged, embarrassed by the back-handed compliment. "I'm not some people. Besides, performing is an important part of my life. I'd be lost without it."

Briggs thought for a moment before he nodded. "Okay, here's what I'd like you to do. You stick to your routine, do exactly what you would have been doing if everything was normal. I'll tag along to keep an eye out, but I'll try to be as unobtrusive as possible. With a little luck, Chumpster and the others will think they were seen by a woman guest, not somebody on staff."

Provided, of course, that no one told them otherwise. That was the downside of the situation, but there was a more optimistic aspect, too. If Dickinson's killers were dumb enough to come sniffing around the Red Rooster for information, they could easily tip their hand to Briggs, who would be only too happy to deal with them.

"I've got a few hours before I need to get ready," Elsabeth said. "Ordinarily I'd do some gardening."

"Go ahead," Briggs said. "I need to take a better look around, anyway."

She turned off the soup and left it to cool as she went to get her gardening tools. When she came back wearing a floppy straw hat, work gloves, and bright yellow "gators" on her feet, Briggs couldn't help but grin.

"That's some outfit," he said.

Elsabeth laughed. "The very latest from *Feed and Seed*. Let it never be said I'm not fashionable."

He shook his head, marveling at a woman who was so beautiful and yet so unpretentious. The women he'd known had been far more absorbed with their appearance. Elsabeth seemed to like making fun of it. But then, she did spend a great deal of her time convincing people they were seeing something that wasn't real. Under those circumstances, it would be tough not to decide that appearances didn't count for much.

He left her to her gardening while he scouted around the house. As Elsabeth had warned, the ground dropped off sharply in three directions but it wasn't immediately obvious. First there were the gardens and lawns bracketed by evergreens and rhododendrons. These effectively screened what had been the quarry. If he hadn't known the drop-offs were there, they would have surprised him.

But there they were. On the far side of the trees he could see how the earth had been gouged to create a chasm covering at least twenty or thirty acres. Over time, small plants and bushes had grown in between the hard gray granite and a few tiny streams had even found their way into the hollow. What must once have been unsightly was now perfectly pleasant. Except for anyone who happened to tumble into it unaware. Then the bushes and plants wouldn't count for much. Only the hard-edged rock and the long, lethal drop would matter.

He went back to the house thoughtfully. Automatically he noted the number of ground-floor windows, sixteen, and doors, three. Besides the main entrance, there was a side door that led into the living room and a back door that led to the kitchen. There was also a set of outside steps to the basement that were covered with folding wooden doors. All of the windows and doors were wired to the security system. Whoever had installed it had known what he was doing.

Satisfied that the house was as secure as possible, Briggs went in search of Elsabeth. She was on her knees in front of what he took at first glance to be a vegetable garden until he realized there were no vegetables in sight.

"What's all this?" he asked, looking at the neat rows of plants waving in the soft breeze.

"This and that," Elsabeth said. She had a streak of dirt on her nose and several stray wisps of hair had come loose from under her hat. Her work gloves were muddy and there were soil stains on her knees. She looked relaxed, happy, and very beautiful.

He bent down beside her and reached out a hand to touch the delicate sprigs of leaves closest to him.

"Which is this . . . or should I say, that?"

Elsabeth laughed. It was a soft, unaffected sound alive with good humor and intelligence. "That's thyme, next to it is parsley. These are chives and this is oregano.'' She plucked a leaf from one of the as yet unnamed plants and held it up to him. "Here, taste.''

Gingerly he bit. Instantly a delicate, refreshing taste settled over his tongue.

"Lemon mint,'' Elsabeth said. "It makes a delicious tea as well as a flavoring for lamb.''

"Amazing,'' Briggs said. He was genuinely impressed. Gardening had always been a mystery to him. The notion that people could draw such things from the earth had very little relevance to the concrete jungles where he'd lived most of his life. Now he was beginning to suspect what he'd missed.

"What's that?'' he asked, pointing to a tall, stately-looking plant that was growing a little removed from the others. It was made up of a vibrant, bell-shaped flower that grew in clusters along a slender stem.

"That's foxglove,'' Elsabeth said. She stood up and dusted off her knees.

"Do you cook with that, too?''

She cast him a quick glance, as though trying to judge whether or not he was serious. Deciding that he was, she said, "No, foxglove is a medicinal plant. The active ingredient in it is digitalis.''

Digitalis he'd heard of; his father had been on it for several years before the final heart attack that killed him. But he'd had no idea that it came from such a pretty, innocent-appearing plant.

On a hunch, he bent down again and examined the separate row in which the foxglove grew. "What's this one?'' he asked, pointing to a smaller, less dramatic plant with long leaves and a pale, veined flower.

Elsabeth brushed clumps of dirt off her tools and put them back in the basket before she replied.

"Henbane. The oil taken from its leaves is good for rheumatism. Georgette suffered from that as she grew older. She found the old remedy more effective than what the doctors prescribed."

"Henbane..." Briggs frowned. Foxglove he hadn't heard of, but henbane he'd come across. Back in the early 1970s he'd worked with a tactical drug unit attached to college campuses. He remembered the unit's supervisor talking about the long history of hallucinogens, how, far from being invented by the hippies, they'd been an important part of cultures all over the world. They'd often been used in religious ceremonies including those of the medieval witches who achieved their fabled broom flights by rubbing ointments on their bodies that made them feel as though they could fly. Ointments made from common, garden-variety substances such as . . . henbane

"Your great-aunt had interesting tastes," Briggs said.

Elsabeth murmured something noncommittal and headed for the house.

"I've got to get cleaned up," she said over her shoulder. "Dinner's in half an hour."

Chapter 5

Briggs stayed outside a while longer. The sun was slanting to the west and the air was cooler than it had been during most of the day. It was pleasant in the garden even though he eyed the plants with heightened caution.

He was taking a closer look at a low, scrubby tree when the hairs at the back of his neck rose slightly. Automatically his hand went to the small of his back as he whirled around.

Twin pairs of green eyes blinked at him in surprise.

"Oh," said a small, freckled boy.

"Hi," said the little girl at his side.

"Who're you?" Briggs asked. He was feeling more than a little foolish standing there with a gun in his hand staring down at children. He put the weapon away hastily.

"I'm Johnny," the boy said. He eyed the gun with disturbing calmness. Too much TV, Briggs figured.

"I'm Jacey," the girl added, equally unflutterable. "Who're you?"

"My name's Briggs." He looked from one to the other. He didn't know a whole lot about kids but he guessed they were about six years old. In addition to the green eyes, both had light blond hair, turned-up noses, full mouths and gently rounded chins. Each was slender with long, coltish legs. They both wore khaki pants and T-shirts, Johnny's being blue and Jacey's red. Except for the superficial difference of their sex, they were identical.

"You're twins."

Johnny nodded. "We're the Cavendish twins." He stated this as though naming a recognized phenomenon of nature, something anyone in the area should be well acquainted with.

"Do you live near here?" Briggs asked, wondering just where they had come from without his being aware of them.

Jacey gestured toward the road. "We live across the way. Elsabeth lets us visit. Are you a friend of hers?"

"You could say that," Briggs replied. "I'm staying here for a while."

"You know about the garden?" Johnny asked.

"I'm learning."

"You have to be very careful here," Jacey said. "You never touch anything unless Elsabeth says it's okay because there are some things here that could hurt you even though they look real pretty."

"I'll remember that," Briggs said solemnly. He didn't know much about kids, but these two seemed nice enough. Bright and levelheaded, polite, easy to get along with . . .

Jacey crooked her finger, urging him closer. He crouched down, thinking that they really were cute. Just like the kids in the old television shows where the biggest thing they ever had to worry about was whether Dad would let them keep the puppy or build a tree house.

"Elsabeth's a witch," Jacey said. Her eyes were very wide. She looked like a small, solemn pixie.

"Don't you mean she's a magician?" Briggs asked gently.

Jacey shook her head. "No. That's what people think but we've seen her." She glanced at her brother, who took up the story.

He leaned closer to Briggs and, with his voice suitably lowered, said, "We peeked."

Briggs's eyebrows rose. "You did? Why?"

The twins nodded in unison. "We know it was wrong but we didn't mean to do it. We were playing ball and it rolled into the garden. When we went to get it, we saw Elsabeth in the kitchen doing the *real* magic, not the stuff she does at the Red Rooster. Zared was helping her."

"Who's Zared?" Briggs asked because that seemed the safest response.

"The cat," Johnny said. Importantly he added, "His name means ambush. That's when somebody sneaks up on you and—"

"I know what ambush means," Briggs said. "It's a good name for him." He stood up and looked at them both bemusedly. They were nice kids and they seemed smart enough, but they wouldn't do Elsabeth any good by letting their imaginations run away with them.

"You know," he said, "if you tell people that Elsabeth does real magic, some of them might get the wrong idea."

"We know that," Johnny said. "We only told you because you're her friend. We'd never tell just anyone."

"Did you tell your parents?" Briggs asked.

The twins nodded.

"What did they say?"

"That Elsabeth is a very nice person but that she doesn't do anything really strange," Johnny replied. "They took us to see her magic show. It was neat."

"But not as neat as the stuff she did in the kitchen," Jacey said.

Briggs suppressed a sigh. There didn't seem much point in trying to convince them they hadn't seen anything that couldn't be rationally explained. After all, they were just kids.

They looked at him solemnly. "We have to go home now," Johnny said. "We just wanted to know who you were."

"Daddy says Elsabeth was really pretty," Jacey offered, "and he wondered why she didn't have a boyfriend but Mommy said she shouldn't be in any rush 'cause there's more to life than just men." She paused an instant for breath before adding, "But they'll both still be glad to hear about you."

While Briggs was still digesting this, they darted off, pausing only long enough to look both ways on the road before disappearing behind a hedge.

He was left with the odd sense that he had encountered the white rabbit—twin version. That bit about Elsabeth not having a boyfriend was interesting, though. It confirmed his own opinion of her as self-reliant and independent.

Yet she had thanked him for making her feel safe.

He sighed for real this time, stuck his hands in his pockets and ambled into the house. Elsabeth was in the kitchen putting the final touches on dinner. She glanced over her shoulder and smiled.

"I ran into your neighbors," Briggs said. "The short, freckled ones."

The smile deepened. "How are Johnny and Jacey today?"

"They seem fine. They also say you're a witch."

A slow flush spread over her cheeks. She turned back to the counter. "They're just children."

"Hmm. Anything I can do to help?"

Without looking at him again, she shook her head. "No, thanks, everything's about ready. Why don't you get comfortable?"

A novel idea. He was used to a lot of things with women but comfort wasn't one of them. However, he was willing to give it a try.

"This smells great," he said a short time later when she had set out bowls of the soup. Even though it was cold, he could make out the mingled scents of red pepper, chicken stock, and something else he couldn't quite identify.

"What is the secret ingredient?" he asked.

She sat down next to him, demurely unfolded her napkin and dropped it into her lap. The gaze she slanted him was filled with gentle humor. "You mean the secret, *witchy* ingredient?"

"That's the one."

"Pear. Nobody ever thinks of it, but a nice ripe pear—preferably Bartlett—adds a silky texture to the soup and offsets the tartness of the red pepper."

"Actually that was going to be my first guess."

"Hmm."

The soup was as delectable as its appearance promised. It was followed by cold poached chicken and a Bibb lettuce salad. For a man who had been living—more or less—on fast-food hamburgers, Briggs more than did justice to it.

He sat back replete, thinking that this wouldn't be at all hard to get used to. A beautiful, enticing woman who somehow wove a web of comfort around her, fantastic food, a quaint old house, peace and quiet. What more could a man ask for?

Before he could let himself get too specific about that, Elsabeth said, "There's dessert if you'd like, crème caramel."

Briggs seriously considered it but the thought of the extra push-ups he already had to do dissuaded him. Instead he cleared the dishes away while Elsabeth got ready for work. The kitchen might look like something from another century with its rough-hewn beams hung with bunches of drying flowers and the big, handwoven baskets on top of the cabinets, but it boasted a state-of-the-art dishwasher. He had everything shipshape by the time Elsabeth came back down.

In the interest of keeping her routine as normal as possible, they took both cars. Briggs waited while Beelzebub coughed and complained, snorted and stalled, and finally started up. He followed at a respectful distance.

They parked behind the restaurant and went in through the kitchen. Mike was there, supervising the setting up. He looked surprised to see them.

"You sure you want to work tonight?" he asked Elsabeth.

She nodded. "There's no reason why I shouldn't...at least, so long as it's all right with you."

"It's better than all right," Mike assured her. "You know if you're not here, people'll be asking me all night why not." He turned to Briggs. "You expectin' any trouble?"

Briggs shook his head. "I'm just here to keep Elsabeth company."

Whether Mike believed that or not, he didn't say. Elsabeth excused herself to get ready. When she was gone, Mike said, "I'll show you around."

Briggs was glad the restaurant owner didn't have to have everything spelled out for him. They walked into the main part of the building, a large taproom that would seat forty plus another dozen at the bar. There were also two dining rooms and a private room used for parties. It would be empty that night.

Briggs did the usual check of the doors and windows. There was one entrance in the front and two on each side, all unlocked as prescribed by the fire code. Two others were in the kitchen. The kitchen was reached by a corridor running off the taproom. Another hall led to the rest rooms.

"You expecting much of a crowd?" Briggs asked.

"We run full-up on Saturdays. Didn't always used to be that way, but Elsabeth's a big draw. You ever caught her act?"

"Just one or two tricks," Briggs said. He still hadn't figured out how she'd done that thing with the flowers. There had to be a straightforward explanation. Magic took a lot of cleverness and hard work but it wasn't . . . *magic.*

"She'll knock your eyes out," Mike said. "I've been watching her for weeks now trying to see how she does it and I don't have a clue. Far as I can tell, it's just what she says it is—magic."

Briggs refrained from making any comment. When Mike left him on his own a while later, he wandered around a little, making sure he had the layout in his head. He picked out a table at the back and staked out the chair directly next to the wall. It had been a long time since he'd allowed himself to sit with his back exposed in a public place. That was just one of the legacies of working the drug detail.

The restaurant began to fill up a short time later. People came in clumps. Most had reservations. The few who didn't and got there early were seated, but before very long, Mike was turning people away. When Elsabeth appeared, a stir ran through the diners and there was a quick smattering of applause. Apparently many of those on hand had seen her magic act before and were eager for more.

Briggs saw why. She worked quickly and smoothly, going from table to table with a smile, a bow, and a grab bag of astonishment. Cards appeared, disappeared and reappeared, often from behind unsuspecting ears. Watches and bracelets wandered from their owners, always unnoticed, only to be returned in due course. Watching how deftly Elsabeth separated people from their property, it occurred to Briggs that she would make a hell of a pickpocket. Either that or a confidence man—woman—because she made the most outlandish and improbable event look perfectly real. Silk scarves flew in profusion only to vanish in the blink of an eye. A twenty dollar bill was folded and torn into tiny bits—to the discomfort of the man who had provided it—only to turn up unfolded and whole. Coins—nickels, dimes, quarters—danced across the table, bent themselves in the middle and bowed to their audience. As a grand finale, she produced a cloud of mauve smoke seemingly from her fingertip. From the smoke there emerged three inflated balloons, two lit sparklers and a burst of confetti.

The applause was sustained as Elsabeth took a final bow and disappeared herself in the direction of the kitchen. Briggs followed. He found her sitting at the counter, looking flushed and happy, holding a glass of ice water in her hand.

"You were great," he said sincerely, hoping he didn't sound too much like one of her awestruck fans, but wondering how he could avoid it.

"Thanks," Elsabeth murmured. She was trying hard not to stare at him but wasn't having much luck. All through the performance she'd been vividly aware of him watching her. It hadn't made any difference that half-a-hundred other people were, too. It was Briggs she kept thinking of when she should have been concentrating on the act.

If only he weren't so flat-out handsome, this devastating man who was living in her house, sleeping in her guest room, invading her dreams. It was all that thick black hair tinged with silver, those deep-set pewter eyes with their absurdly long lashes, the assertive Roman nose and the slashing cheekbones, not to mention the hard, tantalizing mouth and the chin with that little cleft she imagined would just fit the tip of her tongue.

And that was just his head. There was also that infinitely masculine, unabashedly tantalizing body, all six feet plus of it from the linebacker shoulders to the narrow waist and muscled thighs and...

As Great-aunt Georgette would have said, "Oh, heavens."

Georgette had also made a lot of other more interesting comments abut men but Elsabeth didn't want to think about them just then.

"Thanks," Elsabeth murmured. Not exactly a scintillating response but she was stone cold out of anything that resembled wit. A wisp of red-gold hair had fallen across her forehead. She brushed it away impatiently. "There's a good crowd tonight."

"Mike says you pack them in every night."

Elsabeth shrugged. "People like this sort of thing. Even after all they've been exposed to on television and in the movies, close-up magic can still wow them."

Briggs settled on the stool next to her. He was conscious of her faint, elusive perfume and of the hidden, golden gleam of her hair. All around them the bustle and clatter of the kitchen went on, yet they might just as well have been alone. She lifted the glass of ice water to her lips and he noticed that her hands, while slender and smooth, looked strong. The nails were cut short and left unpolished. He supposed that might have something to do with her work and her penchant for gardening.

For a woman remarkably free of pretense, she was extraordinarily adept at it. He thought again of some of the tricks she had performed and wondered at her ability to reshape reality to her own ends.

"Some of what you do," he said, "looks flat-out impossible. It's as if the laws of nature were suddenly suspended. Have you ever been in a situation where somebody got upset by that?"

Elsabeth shook her head. "The worst I ever get is that a person will become very withdrawn, not say anything, maybe even stop watching the performance. That's when I know I've inadvertently hit a nerve and back off. There are people who just can't deal with any challenge to their own version of reality."

He wasn't quite that far gone, but he had to admit that between his close encounter with the boonies, a.k.a. nature, and now this unnerving exposure to a woman who made him feel things he had thought were closed off forever, reality was taking some unexpected turns.

"Have you ever done anything," he asked, "that surprised you?"

The question was only half serious. He knew she had to rehearse every move meticulously, so how could she possibly be surprised? But he asked anyway—in the same way he had always asked provocative questions just to see what kind of a response he would get.

Elsabeth hesitated. Slowly she said, "Everything has to be very precise. Practice and repetition are es-

sential. There isn't any room for doubt. And yet..."
She trailed off, looking uncertain.

"Yet what?" Briggs urged gently.

"Nothing really. It's what I said, you practice, you work hard, and it all comes together in the end."

She left it at that but he was certain that she'd been thinking of something else. Her unwillingness to open up to him troubled him more than it should have. He had always been a very private man, inclined to respect the privacy of others. Yet with Elsabeth he seemed to forget that.

Her second show started a short time later. It went at least as well as the first. The crowd was up for the performance. They clapped and cheered loudly at the end.

Despite their enthusiasm, Elsabeth was tired by the time it was over. Normally, performing energized her, but she had slept poorly the night before and between that and the strain of Dickinson's murder, she wasn't feeling her usual self. A sense of unresolved business hung over her, dampening her mood.

She and Briggs left the restaurant soon after. Once again he waited while she got Beelzebub going. She was grateful for the quiet solidity of his presence. Seeing his headlights in her rearview mirror as she drove along the dark winding roads made her think of how long she had been alone. Ever since Georgette's death, she had fallen into the habit of taking care of herself without thinking that she might be carrying it to extremes. Briggs was making her see things differently.

His car pulled into the driveway directly behind hers. She unlocked the front door, but he went in first and turned off the alarm system. At his instruction, she had left all the house lights on. Everything appeared as usual but it was Zared's slow, deliberate scrutiny that convinced her nothing untoward had occurred. If it had, the cat would have been the first to complain.

"I don't know about you," Elsabeth said to Briggs, "but I'm a little too keyed up to sleep. Would you like a drink?"

"Sounds good to me," he said, knowing that there was no possibility of him sleeping anytime soon.

She gave him a quick smile as she headed for the kitchen.

Chapter 6

Briggs held the brandy bottle in his hand as he read the label. Most of it was in French, with which he had only a passing acquaintance, but he could make out the year clearly enough. It had been bottled when he was in sixth grade. He tried to remember what he'd been doing then—thinking about girls, lusting after a ten-speed Italian racer, dodging his father when the old man had too much whiskey in him. Meanwhile, monks in a winery in France had been blending the brandy he would drink twenty-four years later in the backwoods of Connecticut sitting on a couch with a beautiful magician.

Life was full of things like that.

"Georgette really went for the good stuff, didn't she?" he murmured, savoring his own contentment as much as the pleasantly fiery liquid he was consuming.

"Only the best," Elsabeth agreed. "She didn't think there was much point to anything else."

"A woman of style."

"And substance."

Briggs raised his glass, a Waterford crystal goblet of intricate design and clarity. "Here's to Georgette, wherever she is."

"And whatever she's up to," Elsabeth added. Through her glass she stared at the fire, watching the light shatter into a multitude of colors. With the fading of day, the temperature had dropped sharply enough to make a small fire pleasant. Zared was stretched out in front of it, taking up most of the hearth rug. He had purred violently until he fell asleep. Now he was snoring.

"Was he Georgette's cat?" Briggs asked.

"She would have said he's his own cat, but he did live here with her. I guess I inherited him, too."

"You said you used to visit here, but where did you live before? I mean once you grew up?"

"Here and there," Elsabeth said. She caught his chiding look and laughed. "I know, I have a tendency to answer questions unhelpfully. It's not deliberate, really. It's just that up until recently my life tended to be pretty unsettled."

Losing her parents when she was twelve years old would certainly have contributed to that, Briggs thought. But he wondered what had influenced her more recently.

"I used to spend a lot of time on the road," Elsabeth explained when he asked. "I'd be in Las Vegas for a few weeks, then go to Los Angeles, maybe do a gig on one of the cruise ships on the Pacific run. Then I'd head back to New York, play some of the clubs there, go down to Atlantic City and hit the cruise ships for the Caribbean. In between, I toured the Midwest—Chicago was always great—and I'd have something every year in Texas, both Houston and Dallas. Every other year I'd tour in Europe and I played Japan several times. It was a really hectic way to live but I enjoyed it for a while."

Briggs was trying hard not to stare at her openmouthed. Elsabeth laughed gently. "Don't be too impressed. Usually if you're a professional magician, you have to tour, there's just no two ways about it. Besides, Georgette helped me a lot in the beginning, and having a family name that was known didn't hurt, either. I definitely got some breaks."

"You must also have been very good," Briggs said.

Elsabeth shrugged. "I worked hard and I really loved what I was doing. It's tough to screw up when you've got that much going for you."

"Why did you stop?"

"I found that what I really liked best was developing new acts, so that's most of what I do now." She put her drink down and held out a hand. "I'm working on a couple of tricks right now. Would you like to see them?"

Briggs swallowed hastily. The last time a young woman had smiled at him quite so invitingly, "tricks" had also been the subject of conversation. So had the two hundred dollars she'd wanted. Briggs remembered how annoyed she'd been when he'd flashed his badge.

"Sure," he said as he stood up.

A narrow, curving staircase led to the second floor. At the top was a small hallway furnished with a low table and a pottery vase filled with daisies. Briggs had already realized that the house appeared deceptively small from the outside when it was in fact generously proportioned. He wasn't surprised to see that there were four rooms upstairs. The doors to three of them stood open. Through one he glimpsed a high, pencil-post canopy bed that appeared to be draped in white gauze. Another gave onto a large bath and a third led to what looked like a study. Elsabeth opened the fourth door.

"I keep this closed to discourage Zared," she explained. She frowned slightly as she added, "Not that it always works. Somehow he manages to come and go as he pleases."

She flipped on the lights to reveal a room that was not only large but also more than double the usual height. The ceiling soared, which was fortunate because otherwise there wouldn't have been room for the guillotine.

Guillotine?

"Is that . . . ?" Briggs asked.

"Sure is," Elsabeth said. "Georgette kept it as a souvenir."

"Of what? The Reign of Terror?"

"She wasn't that old," Elsabeth chided. She walked over to the deadly apparatus and patted it affectionately. "This was the prop used in what was probably the greatest trick Georgette ever did, the 'Severed Head Routine.' It was a showstopper every time."

"I can imagine," Briggs muttered. The blade was hoisted to the top of the guillotine in the ready position. Looking up at it, he could have sworn he saw rusty stains that looked uncannily like real blood. "Nice trick. How did it work?"

"I don't know."

He turned and looked at her. She was still wearing her magician's getup and had her hands thrust into the trouser pockets. Her russet hair drifted unbound around her face. Her head was tilted slightly to one side. She looked a little tired, thoughtful, and flat-out gorgeous.

"*You* don't know?"

She shrugged. "Georgette left it to me as sort of a challenge. She said I'd figure it out eventually but if I don't, the answers are in a sealed letter she also left."

"You've been trying to solve it for a year?"

"Off and on. I've had other things to do, too."

"Are you close?"

"I don't think so."

"Aren't you tempted to read the letter?"

Elsabeth looked genuinely surprised. "Of course not. That would spoil all the fun."

The fun of figuring out how an instrument of atrocious death could be turned into a magician's toy. That came under the heading cops knew well: different strokes for different folks. Up to a point.

"You couldn't get hurt, could you?"

"Not unless I stick my head under it, which, believe me, I'm not about to do."

Mildly reassured, Briggs allowed his attention to be drawn to a large transparent cabinet that sat in the middle of the room. It was made entirely of clear Plexiglas and was hinged on one side.

"Disappearing acts are a dime a dozen," Elsabeth said. "They're all done pretty much the same way, with false bottoms or sides that conceal whatever's doing the disappearing, or hidden doors that allow the subject to sneak out."

Briggs was walking all the way around the cabinet. Whichever way he looked, he could see right through. "You couldn't hide or sneak out of this one."

Elsabeth nodded. "Sure looks that way, doesn't it? But watch."

She stepped into the cabinet, smiled at him, and waved. Instantly the cabinet began to fill with smoke. For several seconds his view was entirely obscured. When the smoke cleared, Elsabeth was gone.

Every nerve in Briggs's body went into full alert. He jumped forward and wrenched open the door. There was a lingering hint of smoke but otherwise it was empty.

This couldn't be happening. He'd been staring right at her. The cabinet was transparent. There was no place for her to have gone. Quickly he felt down all sides of the cabinet, confirming that there were no hidden panels. Only then did he realize what he should have seen from the beginning. The bottom was solid. It hid the floor beneath it.

Muttering under his breath, he took hold of the cabinet and maneuvered it several inches to the side. That was far enough to confirm his hunch. Beneath the cabinet was a trapdoor.

Briggs sighed. He put the cabinet back where it belonged and went downstairs. Elsabeth was sitting on the couch in front of the fire. She grinned at him.

"Sometimes the classics are the best," she said.

"Trapdoors are classic?" Briggs asked, trying not to look too relieved now that he'd found her. She seemed no worse for wear.

"Absolutely, and magicians love them."

"You set me up with all that talk about hiding inside the cabinet or sneaking out."

"The patter's part of the trick. If you remember, I warned you about that yesterday."

True enough. "How'd you do the smoke?" he asked.

"There's a lever built right into the floor. It activates a small cartridge at the same time that the cabinet bottom drops open, pushing the trapdoor in the process."

"Neat. Would you mind also explaining how this house happens to have a trapdoor on its second floor? There are easier ways to get downstairs, after all."

The question seemed to surprise her. He half expected her to ask if there was something unusual about such means of impromptu entry and exit. Instead she said, "This house is full of trapdoors. The one in the workroom goes into the pantry behind the kitchen. Now that you mention it, I never did ask Georgette what they were doing here."

"Would she have known?"

"Oh, yes, I think so. She knew a great deal about the house's history. It fascinated her."

Briggs was about to ask how much she'd told Elsabeth when Zared butted between them. He thrust his head against Elsabeth, demanding to be petted. She obliged just as the clock on the mantle chimed.

"It's late," she said. "We'd both better get some rest."

Briggs agreed, even though he was sure he wouldn't sleep. The night before had been a fluke. He'd be awake for hours thinking about Dickinson, the perps and those damned trapdoors. Not to mention the beautiful woman sleeping so near.

Twenty minutes later he was snoring gently.

This time when he awoke there was no weight on his chest. It was still dark—the deep, still darkness of the middle of the night. The house was wrapped in silence, broken only by the sound of something moving through the underbrush immediately outside the house.

Briggs was on his feet, gun in hand, in less time than it took to draw breath. In the short time he had spent in the house, his brain had automatically recorded the position of the floorboards and stairs that squeaked. He avoided them all without any sense of surprise, it was simply how he functioned. In the hallway he stood motionless for several seconds, listening to the night sounds. Upstairs there was silence. He had to hope that Elsabeth was still safely asleep. Downstairs there was no indication that the house had yet been penetrated, but the movements from outside were unmistakable. They were also coming closer.

Swiftly he ran down the hallway and into the kitchen, where he paused, gun ready, watching the back entrance. Nothing. Only the same persistent rustles from outside. Whoever it was, they weren't taking any chances. Too bad they had no way of knowing there was a cop, awake and armed, waiting for them on the other side of the door.

Not that he was prepared to wait all night. He was hungry for these guys, wanted them *bad*. There was only a slim chance they might change their minds and decide to hightail it, but he wasn't going to take that risk.

His right hand held the pistol. With his left hand he took hold of the doorknob. At the same instant that he twisted it, he flicked the wall switch with his shoulder. Immediately light flooded the kitchen and the walkway outside.

Briggs threw open the door. He stood in shooting stance, knees bent, arms out. Except for his boxer shorts, he was naked.

"Don't move! Police!"

Upstairs, Elsabeth woke with a start. She'd been in the midst of the nicest dream, something about lying on a sun-drenched beach with Briggs at her side...

Police?

"What on earth?" she murmured as she jumped out of bed and ran for the door. She reached the kitchen. A very large, almost naked man was standing in the door holding a gun on...

Two terrified raccoons.

"Briggs, no!"

Elsabeth launched herself across the room, thumping straight up against what felt like a combination of granite and steel. Briggs's arm shot skyward, the gun went off, and a shower of plaster rained down on them both.

The raccoons disappeared. Undoubtedly they had better things to do.

"Damn it!" Briggs stared down at her in disbelief. He looked positively livid. "That is the *stupidest* thing I have ever seen anyone do! Throw yourself at a cop with a gun? Really smart, Elsabeth. Do you have any idea what could have happened?"

The gall of the man! He was the one who had been about to commit a heinous crime against two helpless animals. He was the one running around the house in the middle of the night in just his undershorts—which she absolutely was not going to think about. He was the one shooting out her ceiling, as though genuine plaster grew on trees these days. Just who did he think he was, anyway?

"Do I have any idea? What're you, out of your mind? They were raccoons, for God's sake! They weren't going to hurt anything."

Briggs lowered his gun. He had the grace to look sheepish, but only a little.

"How was I supposed to know that? I woke up and heard something outside the house. For all I knew it could have been Chumpster and his pals come to finish the job. What was I supposed to do? Just lie there in bed until they clarified their intentions?"

Mentioning bed wasn't smart. It reminded him that she was wearing a filmy baby-doll nightie that barely reached the top of her thighs. Her hair was loose and tumbled around her shoulders. Her face was flushed and her eyes looked huge and luminous. She was spitting mad, outraged by the situation and by him.

"Don't you think before you do anything?" she demanded. "I know those raccoons, they come by all the time. I feed them. If you'd shot them, I don't know what I would have..."

Briggs did the only thing a sensible man could do in such a situation. He reached out, put a strong arm around her, and pulled her close.

"Shut up," he said, very clearly and firmly.

Just to drive home the point, he kissed her.

A simple kiss, nothing special. Strictly run-of-the-mill, dime-a-dozen, seen one, seen 'em all...

Baloney.

Elsabeth was a lady accustomed to the unusual—sparklers appearing out of nowhere, lavender smoke and lights, people oooing and ahhing. Nothing fazed her. Until now.

Briggs was the closest thing to unshockable, a street-wise cop who had also done a turn or two on the romance merry-go-round. Nothing surprised him. Until now.

It was just a kiss. But it was also the kind of kiss that set rockets off, caused explosions of light and feeling, made hearts thud out of control, and brought bodies surging together. And in the midst of it all, you could practically hear Mother Nature cackling to herself as she set the hapless humans dancing to her tune.

Just a kiss.

Which begged the question of exactly what would happen when they got to the main event.

When, not if. Because in the split second it took to determine that he had never experienced anything like this before in his life, Briggs made up his mind that they *would* get to the main event. He had, in fact, never heard that such heart-stopping, brain-numbing, life-affirming, preconception-blasting passion even existed. Come hell or high water, he was not going to let the beautiful, tantalizing Elsabeth Grace waltz out of his life. Or more correctly in her case, "go poof."

For her part, Elsabeth was nowhere near to disappearing. She was too busy going up in flames. The touch of his mouth, the brush of his tongue on hers, the rough velvet texture of his skin all combined to send her senses ricocheting into some happy never-never land. Sweet, hot languor filled her right along with the seeping realization that she was in Big Trouble. Capital B, capital T, the real thing at long last. She didn't know whether to rejoice or run as fast as she could in the opposite direction. All the time she'd been waiting for the real thing to come along, she'd never imagined it would be packaged in a six foot plus ornery street cop with an aversion to her beloved boonies and eyes that seemed to see right through her.

One of these days, as soon as she got the chance, she was going to have a real heart-to-heart with Mother Nature. Somebody had to straighten that lady out.

At the moment, however, all Elsabeth could think of was extricating herself from a situation that was rapidly getting out of control.

"Briggs," she said softly when she managed to part her lips from his.

"Hmm?"

"I'm not going to bed with you."

"Wanna bet?"

"The farm." She put a little more distance between them and added, "It may seem outlandish in this day and age, but I don't do that kind of thing."

The inherent contradiction made his head spin. He was holding a warm, barely clad woman in his arms and hearing her say that she was . . . what? What exactly was Elsabeth telling him?

He let go of her and stepped back a pace. "Ah, you're not saying that you're . . ."

She looked him in the eye unflinchingly. "Selective. I am very, very selective. Oh, I admit there seems to be something between us..." Something? That was cute. It was only life, death and everything in between. "But I don't think that's any reason to rush into something we both might regret."

"Wait a minute. How many somethings are there? The something between us and the something we shouldn't rush into and the something you don't do. Have I got them all so far?"

He was enjoying this, the unfeeling brute. Standing there, bare-chested, hands on his hips, grinning fit to beat the band, he was having a flat-out good time. Which just went to show how absolutely *strange* the man could be.

"I am so glad you find this amusing," Elsabeth said stiffly. "As for me, I'm going back to bed. Good night."

She turned, intending to stomp away in proper stiff-backed fashion, only to be stopped by a firm but tender hand on her arm.

"Elsabeth."

It wasn't fair that he had that voice, too, along with everything else. That gentle, caressing, slightly apologetic voice that went right through her.

"What?"

She wouldn't look at him but she knew he was still smiling and suddenly that infuriated her. "Stop it," she said, pushing away from him. "I don't want this to happen. Things are bad enough right now."

He froze, feeling the hurt to the marrow of his bones. But a moment later a balm flowed over it. Understanding.

As his old man would have said, "Wise up." She was scared to death, which under the circumstances was the smart way to be. He was coming on much too hard and much too fast. For some women it would have been okay but it wasn't for her. She was different, unusual . . . special.

"I'm sorry, Elsabeth." He touched her arm lightly, so that she met his eyes. "I really am. You don't have any reason to be scared of me."

"I'm not," she said, startled by the notion. "It isn't you. It's . . . what you make me feel."

Which proved to him beyond any shadow of a doubt exactly how innocent she was, because any woman with an ounce of genuine experience would have known how potent those few little words would be. They just about shot his self-control to hell.

He cleared his throat. "I think maybe you had better go back to bed now."

Elsabeth was not the type of woman who enjoyed being told what to do. Fact was, she could barely tolerate it. But she took one quick, sidelong glance at Briggs and high-tailed it out of there.

Upstairs, lying in bed with the covers pulled up to her chin, she reassured herself that she absolutely was not scared of him. He was only a man, after all, and a nice one to boot.

Too nice. Too intelligent. Too strong and gentle and comforting and steady and trustworthy and . . .

Soft currents of sleep washed her out from the shore of wakefulness into a moon-swept sea where she slumbered amid dreams of love and danger, the two intermingling until she wasn't sure where one ended and the other began.

It was not a restful night.

Chapter 7

"What would you like to do today?" Elsabeth asked. She was being very polite, pouring orange juice and spreading cream cheese on bagels, setting out place mats and napkins, doing everything she could think of to stop her from looking at Briggs.

He was sitting at the kitchen table scanning the newspaper the delivery boy had just dropped off. When he glanced up, he was frowning.

"What?"

She slid a place mat in front of him and put a glass of orange juice on it. "I asked what you wanted to do today. After all, it is Sunday. I don't have to work and I presume you don't want to sit around the house for hours."

"Actually, that wouldn't be a bad idea." He spotted the orange juice, realized what she was doing and got up to help her.

If only he was one of those men who expected to be waited on, but he wasn't. He insisted on doing his share and more, and he had no qualms about crossing any artificial lines that separated "women's work" from what men could be reasonably expected to do.

All in all, he was just about perfect. And he expected her to spend the day with him sitting around the house? Just the two of them?

Right.

"Let's go fishing," she said brightly, making it sound like the greatest idea anyone could have for spending a slow Sunday.

Briggs looked at her as though she'd suggested they flap their wings and fly to the moon. "Do what?"

"Go fishing. You know, bait a hook, dunk it in the water, pull out a fish. Like that."

"Fish comes in little frozen rectangles with breading on it. You get it at the supermarket, stick it in the microwave, put it on a plate. No fuss, no muss."

Elsabeth's eyes widened. "You eat that stuff?"

"Sure, what's wrong with it?"

"Only everything. You need fresh food that hasn't had all the nutrients processed out of it."

Briggs looked offended. "Hey, I get all the nutrition I need. You'll never catch me neglecting any of the main food groups."

"Which are?"

"Coffee, chili dogs, cheesecake and onions."

Elsabeth put down her juice—fresh squeezed with a garnish of mint leaves—and sniffed. "Together?"

"Only on special occasions."

"It's a miracle you've lived this long."

He spread his hands modestly. "Providence moves in mysterious ways."

"I'll say. Well, I've got bad news for you. While you're living here, you're going to eat decently and that includes fresh fish. The reservoir is chock-full. We'll go right after breakfast."

She waited, expecting him to refuse since he was definitely not the kind of man to tolerate being bossed around. But he said nothing, merely looked at her out of those silvery eyes and sipped his coffee. Sunlight flooding in through the windows touched his forearms. Elsabeth resisted the urge to run her fingers over the firm, burnished skin lightly roughened by dark, curling hairs. She was proud of her self-restraint, never mind that it was running out fast.

"I'll give it a try," he conceded finally, making her feel as though she had been allowed a victory she would never have won for herself.

The reservoir was a popular spot, not surprising given that it was surpassingly beautiful. Even Briggs whistled softly as they left the car by the side of the road and walked across the ground strewn with pine needles to the edge of the water.

"It looks like a Scottish loch," he said with a touch of reverence that made her heart tighten.

"Like something out of a dream," Elsabeth murmured. She gazed over the pristine expanse of water dotted by small islands where birds nested, and fringed by a thick barrier of evergreens. No movement marred the surface, swimmers and boaters alike were barred. People who gathered there to fish or walk tended to keep their voices down. There was a cathedral-like hush that further emphasized how rare and precious such a place was becoming.

For a man who wasn't exactly a stranger to violence, Briggs proved disconcertingly squeamish on the subject of worms. It was oddly touching, and Elsabeth had to work hard not to laugh, but try though he did, Briggs couldn't bait a hook. He kept letting the wigglers drop out of his hands onto the soft, moist ground beside the reservoir. True to their name, they wasted no time escaping.

Exasperated, Elsabeth held out her hand. "Give me that. I'll do it."

"Do you have to?" Briggs asked. "I'm not really interested in catching a fish, so what do I need a worm for?"

"You said you'd try," she reminded him sternly. Before he could argue further, she plucked a worm from the bucket and did the necessary.

"See, it isn't hard at all."

"That depends on whether or not you're the worm," Briggs muttered.

"They don't have nervous systems," Elsabeth explained patiently. "They can't feel pain, and besides, worms have short life spans. It's not as though you're depriving them of long, happy years."

Not for anything would she admit that she'd never felt quite right about the worm's fate. But no one had ever said nature was fair. No one sane, anyway.

She glanced behind her back to be sure no one was in the way and swung her arm, casting the line out in a perfect arc. It landed with a plop forty feet or so from the shore.

"Now you try," she said encouragingly. "But don't worry if you don't get it right at first. Casting takes practice."

"Hmm." His powerfully muscled arm moved, the line flew, and . . . perfection. It was getting just a little tiresome.

"You've done this before," Elsabeth said.

"Nope."

"Come on."

"No, it's true." He settled comfortably on a nearby rock and stuck the end of the fishing rod in the ground in front of him. The khaki pants and cotton shirt he wore were similar to the clothes worn by many of the other men, but Briggs somehow looked different. He was bigger, harder, more confident. Even in a completely new situation, he seemed in command.

"Didn't your dad ever take you fishing?" Elsabeth asked as she sat down next to him. She could smell the faint scent of his skin—a combination of after-shave, soap and pure man. He moved slightly and she saw that his brows had drawn together.

"Dad wasn't much interested in that kind of thing. But he did take me to the track."

"Oh . . . he liked horses."

Briggs laughed shortly. "He liked to gamble. The horses were incidental."

Elsabeth had a quick, painful glimpse of the boy Briggs must have been, trailing after his father in places a child should not, aware of human weaknesses a child should not have confronted. "I'm sorry," she murmured.

Briggs turned his head and looked at her hard. "What for? You had nothing to do with it."

"I know, but isn't that what most people say when they hear something like that?"

"You're not most people. You told me yourself."

Which put her neatly on the spot, Elsabeth thought as she prudently turned her attention back to the water. They fished in silence for perhaps fifteen minutes, no longer. Elsabeth tried a couple more casts but the fish seemed disinterested. She was about to suggest that they move to another spot when the line on Briggs's fishing rod suddenly jerked.

"You've got one!"

"Great. If I wait, will it go away?"

Ignoring that, Elsabeth urged him to his feet. "Come on, that's lunch you're being so cavalier about."

Making it clear that he was humoring her, Briggs got up. He took hold of the reel and began bringing the fish in. "This thing's heavy," he said, surprised.

"That's how we want 'em. Keep reeling, don't lose him now."

"How do you know it's a him?" Briggs demanded, his broad shoulders flexing. "Maybe it's a lady fish with a whole gaggle of little fish who will miss mommy something awful."

Elsabeth rolled her eyes. "Anyone ever tell you that you have a tendency to anthropomorphize?"

"Say what?"

"Endow animals with human characteristics they don't actually possess. First jail-bait raccoons, now Mother of the Year trout. So how come you and Zared don't get along better?"

"Because Zared is from another planet, one hostile to our own. He's the advance guard of a wave of spitting fur balls poised to take over every living-room couch, hearth, rug and sunny spot from here to Tierra del Fuego. Besides, he sleeps on my chest and makes me think I'm suffocating. Call me picky, but I don't appreciate that."

"It's just his way of showing he likes you," Elsabeth said cheerfully.

Briggs ignored her. He gave the reel a final few twists and hauled the line out of the water. Tangling from the end of it was the largest trout Elsabeth had ever seen.

"Holy-moly," she said. "That's got to be the granddaddy of them all."

"Big, huh?" Briggs muttered as he bent over the fish. It flopped on the ground, eyeing him balefully.

"There have been stories about a really big trout in these waters, but I never heard of anyone who actually saw him. Talk about beginner's luck."

"I guess so," Briggs said quietly. He reached down and with gentle deftness extricated the hook from the fish's mouth. Picking him up, he walked into the water.

"What are you doing?"

"Putting him back."

"But you caught him fair and square."

"And I'm letting him go fair and square."

"But—"

"No buts," he said firmly as he came back up the bank minus the fish. "If you're that hungry for trout, we'll find a fish market and buy some. But I'm not eating anything that looks like it knows more than I do."

Elsabeth took a step back and gazed at him. "You're a softie."

He flushed slightly. "Am not."

"Are so."

"Am not."

"How can you be so tenderhearted and still have survived all these years as a cop?"

"Try me against something my own size and you'll find out."

Elsabeth was tempted but she was getting used to that. Being around Briggs was like nothing she'd ever experienced. She knew she ought to be worrying about the men she'd identified but she couldn't seem to manage it. With Briggs she felt strangely safe even as he challenged her more than any man had ever done. Figuring out why would be a neat trick, one she didn't feel up to at the moment.

"Why don't we forget about fishing," she suggested, "and just go for a walk?"

Briggs agreed, but reluctantly. A narrow path ran alongside the reservoir. The further it led away from the main road, the more pristine and beautiful the surroundings became. But Briggs showed no sign of appreciating them.

"I don't like this," he muttered. "It's too isolated and too open. We could be in someone's gun sight this very second and we wouldn't know it until it was too late."

Elsabeth grimaced. "Thanks for the cheerful thought. I was just starting to enjoy myself."

He shrugged unapologetically. "You want to come back here some time after this is all settled, fine. I'm sure I'll appreciate it a lot more. But right now, the smart place to be is inside.''

Elsabeth didn't quite know what to make of that. Come back after? That implied a continuing relationship which, heaven knew, she wanted but she hadn't realized he was thinking about, too. Yet hard on its heels was also the reminder that she was in danger. A classic case of good news, bad news.

She was just focusing her mind on that, warily approaching the notion that someone might actually want to kill her, when the possibility was suddenly and hideously reaffirmed.

Boo-om.

Two things happened instantaneously. The ground came up to meet Elsabeth smack in the face and she was all but crushed by a solid weight. Sound reverberated through her, carrying the terrifying echoes of death. Adrenaline surged, her heart raced, and everything else seemed to slow down in painful slow motion.

"Wha—?" She managed to make the sound despite the dirt clogging her mouth. Choking, she spit it out and tried to get her head up so that she could see what was happening.

"Stay down," Briggs said. His voice was at her ear, low and tense, brooking no disagreement. Seconds passed before she realized that he was so close because it was his weight holding her down, his body shielding hers.

"Don't move," he ordered as he lifted off her, pressing a hand to her shoulder for emphasis. "Not a muscle."

Frozen in place by terror greater than any she had ever known, she did not think of disobeying. But temptation proved too great and she did put up her head in time to see him moving swiftly toward the trees, the gun drawn from his leg holster.

He was back before she could do more than imagine half a dozen or so scenarios for his grizzly death. A hand reached out to help her up.

"It was a backfire."

"A what?" she murmured dazedly as she got to her feet.

"A backfire. A car up on the road."

"Oh, my God..." Weakly, she swayed against him. Her face was ashen. Even her lips were colorless. "Briggs..."

"Easy," he murmured as his arms went around her, holding her close to his granite strength. A big hand stroked her hair with rough tenderness. "It's okay, these things happen. It's all over, everything's fine." As he spoke he eased her back to the rocks and sat her down, but did not let her go. She remained cradled in his arms, sheltered from the terrifying face the world had suddenly shown.

Time passed. Gradually Elsabeth became aware of the sun warming her skin, the distant buzzing of insects, the soft breeze blowing off the reservoir. The fear she had felt did not disappear but it did begin to fade like the hues of a painting growing gradually dimmer.

Brighter by far than the terror, more real and lasting was the man who held her. Her cheek rested against the broad curve of his shoulder. Her hands touched his chest, that surface of granite lightly sheathed in velvet. Beneath her thighs she could feel the strength of his muscled legs. He held her with infinite gentleness, yet she was made all the more aware of his strength and will. For a moment the fear threatened to return as she remembered how he had pressed her into the ground, protecting her with his own body.

What if it hadn't been a car's backfire? What if someone had been shooting at them? What if . . .

She raised her head and looked at him. Behind the crown of raven hair, the sky appeared unnaturally bright, as though the world had come more sharply into focus. "Briggs . . ."

His eyes met hers. Fire danced in the silvery depths, ancient, male, demanding. Elsabeth trembled. She wanted him so much that her own desire frightened her. She moved slightly, suddenly aware that he shared her need. Color suffused her cheeks.

Around them, silence reigned. No sounds came from the road. They had walked far enough to be completely alone. There was only the water moving gently near their feet and the deep, dark shadows of the pines beckoning them.

People put such store in words, Elsabeth thought. Yet it was possible to communicate so effectively without them. She had no doubt Briggs knew exactly what she was thinking when she glanced toward the trees. To lie down with him amid the soft, fragrant pine needles, to strip away the reserve of a lifetime, to give full vent to the passion he made her feel. All that would be heaven and more.

A few swift steps and they would be locked away in a world of their own making. It was so close, so easy, so...

Abruptly Briggs stood. Elsabeth's feet hit the ground with unmistakable clarity.

"Let's go," he said.

Go? Could she possibly have been so wrong? Had her own desire so deluded her that she thought he shared her feelings? Last night everything had seemed so clear but now... All the old uncertainties of her life rose suddenly to haunt her. Despite her looks she had never felt confident with men, had always envied the easy way some women seemed to have with them. Magic had not only been her fascination but also her escape from a reality that so often failed to satisfy. With Briggs, everything had seemed different. But clearly she had presumed far too much. Humiliation twisted through her.

She had to get a grip on herself. *Had to.* What had happened was bad enough, she couldn't let him see how rawly exposed her emotions were.

"Elsabeth."

She heard him but refused to respond. Instead she moved away quickly and actually got several paces before his hand closed on her arm.

With implacable firmness, he said, "Listen to me."

"There's nothing to say," she insisted, staring determinedly over his left shoulder.

"Sure there is. For starters, you're not this dumb."

Her temper flared, spilling anger over the hurt. "Thanks a lot."

"*Listen.* You know how I feel. I made that crystal clear last night. But this isn't the time or the place.

When I make love with you, I want a big, cool bed and no chance of being interrupted, because the way you make me feel, once I start I don't think I could stop if the roof fell in on top of us. And if that isn't enough to convince you, then try this. I also want to be absolutely sure you know what you're doing and why. I don't want any confusion in your mind because it's finally dawned on you that you could actually get killed and you're feeling a little too grateful to the guy in charge of keeping you alive.''

Elsabeth's eyes narrowed ominously. The full, glorious fire of her ancestors' Welsh temper came surging to the fore. ''*Grateful?* You're seriously suggesting I'd go to bed with you out of *gratitude?* You think I don't know my own feelings better than that? Not to mention value myself? Why, you—''

Briggs took a prudent step backwards and grinned at her. ''Go ahead, honey, let it all out. You'll feel better.''

''I will not! Don't you tell me how I'll feel. I'm *grateful* when the mailman realizes I didn't put enough postage on a letter and fixes it for me. I'm *grateful* when somebody brings me something special for my garden. I'm *grateful* for shared recipes and birthday presents and phone calls from old friends. I am *not* grateful for having my existence turned upside down, for being scared out of my wits, and for not knowing if I'm coming or going because some dumb cop from Bridgeport is living in my guest room and messing up my head!''

Briggs ran a hand through his hair, rumpling it endearingly—darn the man!—and said, ''Does he really?''

Elsabeth stared at him. "Does who really?"

"The mailman, does he really put stamps on your letters when you forget to?"

"What has that got to do with . . . ?"

"I never heard of a mailman doing anything like that. It must come from working in the boonies."

"It comes from his being a nice man. Your problem is that you keep seeing complicated motives in everything and sometimes they just aren't there. Sometimes things really are what they seem."

"Maybe, but it's tough for a dumb cop to always know when that is."

"I'm sorry," Elsabeth murmured. "That was out of line. But," she added quickly, "I stand by the rest of it. Now, if you'll excuse me, I'm going home."

She turned on her heel and marched away, telling herself she was hearing things. Briggs wouldn't—couldn't—have chuckled. The man had to have better survival instincts than that.

Didn't he?

Chapter 8

Zared met them at the door when they got back to the house. The cat spared Elsabeth a glance before wrapping himself around Briggs's ankles and purring loudly. Briggs tried to step out of the way but Zared was having none of it. He circled, rumbling contentedly, leaving stray bits of fur clinging to the bottom of Briggs's trousers.

Elsabeth shook her head in disgust. "Cats are supposed to be dignified animals. This one's acting like he got dropped on his head."

Briggs tried to take a step, failed and held up his hands in defeat. "How about helping me out here? I can't move without falling over him."

Elsabeth smiled with just the tiniest bit of maliciousness. "Far be it from me to break up a beautiful relationship. Besides, I've got work to do."

She disappeared up the steps, leaving him to deal with the overly affectionate cat and the emptiness of a long Sunday afternoon.

Or at least she thought she did. When she emerged from her workroom a scant half hour later, driven by equal measures of guilt and boredom, she found Briggs ensconced on the couch in front of the television with Zared curled up beside him.

"What are you watching?" she asked, annoyed that he'd found a way to amuse himself when she couldn't. It was bad enough that she'd dropped her wand twice, but when she fumbled the cards while making a move she'd done only a thousand times or so before, she figured she'd better pack it in.

"Ssh," Briggs said, his attention rapt on the screen.

A crowd of equally absorbed souls stood off on the sidelines while a man in a pink polo shirt and lime-green pants approached a small white ball, wielding a large iron stick.

"Golf," Elsabeth said. "You watch golf?" Her tone made it clear that she thought watching paint dry would be more exciting.

"If you knew anything about the game," Briggs said, without moving his eyes, "you'd be more respectful."

"What's to know? You hit the little ball with the big stick. Either it goes in the hole or it doesn't. Big deal."

The man on the television swung, the ball flew, and the camera followed it up, up, up... Briggs slammed a fist down hard, startling Zared who was not so enamored that he didn't shoot him a chiding look.

"*All right,*" Briggs said. "*Way to go.*"

The crowd was cheering as the commentator babbled excitedly. "What happened?" Elsabeth asked.

"Hole in one. You know what that means?"

"It's pretty obvious. But there is something I've always wondered about. Isn't there a flag in each of the
little holes? If you're pretty close with the ball, somebody takes the flag out, right? But if you've just
started, no one would think to do that so how does the
ball fit in?"

Briggs looked at her for a second to see if she was
joking, decided she wasn't, and said, "Sometimes it
does, sometimes it doesn't. That's part of the game."

"Seems kind of silly to me. Why don't they just
keep the flag next to the hole instead of right in it?"

"Tradition. When the Scots invented the game, they
put the flag in the hole. It's always been that way and
it always will be."

"Traditions," Elsabeth said, "are made to be im-
proved on, if not broken."

"Not in golf." He stood up, spilling Zared onto the
floor, and came toward her. She looked annoyed, disheveled and almost unbearably beautiful. He caught
the faint scent of her perfume and felt the heat coil
within him. It was going to be a long afternoon. "And
not in a few other areas, either. What's for lunch?"

"Frozen pizza."

He repressed a smile. Having a beautiful woman
angry at him because he hadn't made love to her
wasn't the worst thing he'd ever gone through.
"Would you consider defrosting it?"

"I don't see what difference that will make," Elsabeth grumbled. Relenting slightly, she added, "I'll see
what I can do."

Briggs had noticed earlier that Elsabeth did not possess that absolute essential of the modern kitchen, a microwave oven. He therefore wasn't surprised when it took her almost half an hour to return with two plates and a couple of beers. The golf match was still on.

"Do you actually play that?" Elsabeth asked as she set a plate down in front of him.

Briggs shook his head. "Of course not. I'd go nuts inside of five minutes. I watch it when I'm trying to relax." He looked at her pointedly.

"You must do something for exercise." She almost bit her tongue, thinking that she couldn't have been more obvious. But he did have the taut, sculpted body of a man who worked himself hard.

"I play handball," Briggs said. It sounded innocent enough. He saw no reason to tell her that the brand of handball played by him and his friends was as close to lethal as you could get without an actual weapon. It was a hard-driving, no-holds-barred, survival-of-the-fittest workout that chased the demons away for another day and made sleep possible without alcohol or drugs. Some of the guys who played had fallen victim to both at one time or another. Briggs never had but he understood how easy it was to slip.

He took a bite of the pizza. A puzzled look crossed his face.

Elsabeth smiled innocently. "Something wrong?"

He swallowed and shook his head. "No, it's fine. I guess..." He took another bite. "Actually it's excellent. See, you shouldn't be so prejudiced against frozen food. Not when it tastes like this."

"I made it from scratch," Elsabeth said. "The crust is from stone-ground wheat. The sauce is fresh tomato and basil. The sausage comes from a smoke house not far from here and the mozzarella was made by a neighbor of mine. The frozen pizza was only a threat. I'd never actually do that."

"Oh . . ." He took a sip of his beer, eyeing her over the rim of the bottle. It was crisp, light and perfectly chilled. He knew that if he'd wanted it, he could have had a frosted glass. But she'd noticed that he liked beer straight from the bottle so that was how she brought it. No fuss, no muss. Just perfect.

Heaven help him. All that sexy gorgeousness was tough enough but beer the way he liked it *and* great homemade pizza were more than any man could be expected to endure.

"Why," Briggs asked softly, "do I get the feeling that I'm in over my head and sinking fast?"

"Sinking?" Elsabeth repeated innocently. "In what?"

"Good intentions. How come you never got married?"

She recoiled slightly, looking at him with new caution. "Was that handball you said or hardball?"

"Both. It's a legitimate question."

"That could have been phrased a lot more delicately."

"So sue me. I'd still like an answer."

She took a deep breath, steadying herself. "I never got married because I was on the road for years and I saw what happened to people who tried to maintain relationships under those circumstances. Also, I met a lot of men who were nitwits. What about you?"

Score one for her. Ball to him. "I was married," he said. "It didn't work out."

"Why not?"

He thought about that, going over the conclusions he'd come to painfully after the divorce. Finally he said, "We never really got close to each other. We went through all the motions of being married but I never felt like I knew what really made her tick and I'm sure she never felt that way about me. In some important way, we stayed strangers."

"Was she afraid for you?" Elsabeth asked gently.

"Sure, what cop's wife isn't? But I was a cop when she met me and she knew I wasn't going to quit."

Unlike now, Elsabeth thought, when he's only a few weeks away from retirement and a new career as a full-time writer. If that other woman had met him at this point in his life instead of earlier, would the outcome have been different?

"No," Briggs said.

Elsabeth looked up, startled. "I didn't say—"

"I know you didn't but it's inevitable that you'd wonder. Look, don't get me wrong, Patricia has a lot of great qualities. She remarried a few years ago and this time she's really happy. We just weren't meant to be."

"You're very philosophical."

He shrugged. "I'm a realist. People are what they are. They don't change."

"I don't agree," Elsabeth said. "I've seen people change tremendously depending on what happens to them in their lives."

Briggs disagreed but he enjoyed the discussion. The golf match had slipped into the too-usual tedium following that one great shot. He didn't object when, lunch over, Elsabeth suggested they find some other way to amuse themselves.

"How about a game of cards," she suggested. "Gin rummy, poker, pinochle, you name it."

His dark, slashing brows rose in mock dismay. "Play cards with you after I've seen what you can do with a deck? I'd lose my shirt."

It was on the tip of Elsabeth's tongue to say that was fine with her but she restrained herself. Surely the man didn't have her so dizzy with confusion and desire that she couldn't behave like a sensible adult. Or did he?

"Backgammon," she prompted.

"I put myself through the police academy playing that. You really want to take the chance?"

"Guess not. What's left?"

"Chess? I noticed you've got a board."

"Georgette played and she tried to teach me but we didn't get too far."

"Uh-oh," Briggs murmured. "You wouldn't be suckering me, would you?"

Elsabeth's eyes widened. "Who, me?"

They got out the board and set it up. Briggs chivalrously took the black pieces, allowing Elsabeth as white to go first. Play proceeded along fairly predictable lines until suddenly she tried a daring gambit.

"You're putting that knight in danger," Briggs pointed out.

"Let me worry about that."

They played on, not noticing that the light filtering through the curtains had begun to change. Although it was only midafternoon, shadows fell across the garden. Branches moved where before there had been stillness. A wind coming out of the west heralded a change of weather. Thunderclouds followed, blocking out the sun and turning the sky a grayish yellow. A serious storm was on the way.

It began with a sprinkling of rain falling against the windows. Elsabeth looked up, startled. She had been concentrating so intently on the game that she was taken unawares.

"It's raining," she said. Usually, she enjoyed weather like this, but just then it made her feel unexpectedly down, almost depressed. She shivered slightly even though it wasn't cold.

Briggs looked up. "Looks like we're in for a drenching."

They got the windows closed, then settled back into the game but their concentration was broken. The wind had picked up. It moaned around the house. The shutters creaked. Branches swayed in the trees. One of them banged against the house, causing Elsabeth to jump. She knocked against the board, spilling the pieces onto the floor.

"Oh, no."

"It's okay," Briggs said. He went to her quickly but she was already down on her knees, trying to pick up the pieces. Her slender fingers flailed, the pieces slipping from them. Kneeling beside her, Briggs grasped both her hands. "Elsabeth, it's all right."

She shook her head, the curtain of red-gold hair falling forward to obscure her features. Her voice was soft and muffled, tear-filled. "No, it isn't. This is so simple, why can't I do it? What's wrong with me? I'm messing everything up." She choked on a sob.

Briggs cursed under his breath. He let go of her hands but not of her. His powerful arms wrapped her in an embrace that would not be denied. Though she struggled and tried to break free, he would not release her.

"Listen to me," he said urgently, fighting to get through the near-panic that had seized her. "You're scared and you're finally admitting it. There's nothing wrong with that. Stop being so hard on yourself."

"I can't. I have to be strong. There isn't anyone else."

"What about me?" he demanded. Lean fingers curled under her chin, forcing her head up. "Did I just cease to exist?"

"No, of course not, but you're..."

"I'm what?"

"Nothing, it doesn't matter. Just let me go."

"I'm what, Elsabeth? Part of the problem? Is that what you were going to say?"

"Oh, God! I hate this. How dare you know what I'm thinking?"

"You do the same to me."

"No, I don't—" She broke off. He was right, she had done it. The uncanny sense of knowing what he was feeling and thinking had crept over her so that she was hardly aware of it. As naturally as air and light, it had become a part of her being. She had accepted it without a struggle.

She sighed deeply, part relief, part resignation. The red-gold glory of her hair fell away from her face, revealing the purity of her features. Her eyes were wide and luminous, the fear gone from them. They met his candidly.

"Do you want to start the game again?" she said softly.

He watched her lips move, thinking how he had done the same thing the first time he saw her. She had been afraid then, too, having just witnessed Dickinson's abduction. But she had also been strong and determined to do what was right.

"No," he said as his head lowered, darkness against the storm-tossed sky. "No game." His mouth moved on hers, blotting out doubt, banishing hesitation. They clung together, there on the floor amid the scattered pieces of an ancient game. Rain lashed the windows, the wind howled, but they were aware of neither. A far more potent storm had them in its grip.

His hands trembled as they moved along her back, beneath the thin shirt she wore. Her skin was smooth and warm, like silk heated in the sun. Her hips moved against him, making him achingly aware of the need rampaging beyond all control.

A big, cool bed, he had told her. He still had that much control, at least.

Swiftly he stood, lifting her with him. Her arms twined around his neck, he felt the soft rush of her breath against his cheek. The guest room was closest. He took the hallway in rapid strides and kicked the door open. They came down together in the center of the wide bed, arms and legs entwining.

Her hands slipped beneath his shirt to caress the hard, sculpted contours of his chest. She moaned softly as his lips parted hers, his tongue plunging into the sweet depths of her mouth. On fire for him, desperate in her need, Elsabeth twisted on the bed. She had never experienced such an explosion of all her senses. It shattered the safe, known world and tore her from herself.

"Briggs," she whispered, hardly able to breathe before the onslaught of her need, "please..."

He braced himself on his arms and gazed down at her. Her hair spread out over the pillows, framing skin delicately touched by color and lips swollen from the hungry passion of his kisses.

She raised her hand to touch his hard mouth. He caught one finger between his teeth and bit gently. She laughed, her color deepening, and lifted herself. Her tongue lapped softly, with exquisite gentleness, in the hollow of his collarbone and up along the sensitive column of his throat, stroking... stroking... until he could bear it no longer.

Abruptly he was gone from her. Standing beside the bed, he removed his clothes with no pretense at patience. She lay before him, watching with unabashed fascination. Her breasts rose and fell with the agitation of her breathing. His chest, she knew, was broad and taut with muscle, lightly dusted by dark, curling hair. His waist was trim, his hips narrow, and his legs long and hard. The dark hair of his chest extended down his flat abdomen to burgeon round his manhood, springing free and unabashed.

He was perfectly formed, the epitome of everything she desired in a man. But that was not what made her ache for him. Desire was instinctive, subject to the discipline of her mind. It was his gentle strength, his humorous intelligence, his patient caring that shattered the barriers within her.

She rose on the bed, kneeling before him, and quickly stripped off her own shirt. Her bra followed, leaving her naked from the waist up. He cupped her gently in his hands, his thumbs rubbing over her erect nipples. "So beautiful," he murmured as he slipped an arm around her waist, drawing her upright. Swiftly he removed the rest of her clothes, pausing only for an instant before drawing off the final scanty barrier of her panties. Without further hindrance, they came together.

"Elsabeth," he groaned huskily, "I want to wait, I really do, but..."

"Don't," she whispered, her hip arching toward him. "Not this time, not now."

He hesitated a moment longer before the hair-roughened length of his thigh slipped between hers. Open to him, more vulnerable than she had ever been, Elsabeth gloried in her femininity. Her hand found him, learning the proud length of him, drawing Briggs into her.

He drove deeply, withdrew, drove again and again and again. Elsabeth cried out, his name on her lips. He followed as the tightening coils of pleasure shattered, hurtling them both into a realm of incandescent release.

In the aftermath they lay still entwined, dazed and disbelieving. Slowly their heartbeats steadied, their breathing eased. Elsabeth touched his face gently, engulfed in tenderness. This strong, enthralling man had given of himself so completely that the gift still stunned her. Softly she said, "You are so beautiful."

He smiled against her skin. "You're the one who's beautiful. I'm—"

"What?" she demanded teasingly.

"Resourceful?"

"*I'll say.*"

His smile deepened. "Reliable?"

"Extraordinarily."

"A good man in a pinch?"

"Everywhere else, too."

"That gives me an idea."

Her eyes widened as he moved against her, communicating without words exactly what he was thinking of. "You're kidding?"

He raised his head, teeth showing whitely against his burnished skin. "Wanna bet?"

Much later, in the depths of the night as the storm still raged, Elsabeth said softly, "You do understand that I'm not grateful. Limp with passion, extremely impressed and head-over-heels crazy about you, but *not* grateful."

"Understood," Briggs murmured. Talking was almost beyond him but then so was breathing. Where exactly had the idea gotten started that the male was the stronger of the species? Stretched out beside him, wearing only a satisfied smile, Elsabeth looked gorgeous and pleasantly relaxed. By comparison, he was—a wrung-out dishrag gave the general idea.

He sighed deeply and slept, not waking when she pulled the sheet over them both and nestled beside him. The rain against the windows and the smooth rhythm of his breathing followed her into her dreams.

Chapter 9

The ringing phone jarred them both awake. Elsabeth reached out an arm to the bedside table, fumbled and found nothing. Belatedly she remembered where she was. There was no extension in the guest room. She got out of bed, shivering in the early morning coolness. Wrapped in a blanket, she went into the kitchen. Moments later she was back.

Briggs was awake, lying on his back with his arms folded behind his head. The sheet was pushed down to his waist, revealing the broad expanse of his chest. Elsabeth flushed slightly. She had a vague recollection of sleeping all night curled against him.

"It's Lieutenant D'Angelo," she said. "He needs to speak with you."

Briggs didn't react immediately. He lay there, looking at her. "Everything all right?" he asked.

"He didn't say. He—"

"Not with Sal. With you."

Her flush deepened. "I'm fine. I—"

He held out a hand. "Come here."

She gestured vaguely toward the kitchen. "The lieutenant—"

"Can wait."

Her hand slipped into his. He drew her down on the edge of the bed. Holding her eyes with his, he turned her hand palm up and kissed it gently. The caress sent heat racing through her. He laughed and tugged lightly, tumbling her onto the bed. She lay, tangled in the blanket, watching as he stood up. Heedless of his nudity, he said, "Don't go away. I'll be right back."

He left her with a smile but by the time he reached the kitchen, his face was grim.

"What's up?" he said into the receiver.

"A dishwasher at the Red Rooster's gone AWOL," Sal replied, equally curt. Neither man had the time or inclination for pleasantries. "Didn't show up for work yesterday evening and when the owner called his place, there was no answer. Ditto this morning. The guy could be sleeping off a bender at his girlfriend's or dodging bookies or..."

"Or counting his money a thousand miles from here," Briggs concluded.

"Yeah."

"I'm pulling her out," Briggs said flatly.

"Hold on. She made it clear she wanted to stay."

"I don't care what she made clear. We're going."

"You won't get far."

Briggs was silent for a long moment. His voice deathly cold, he asked, "What does that mean?"

Sal hesitated. Static danced up and down the phone line. "Look, for all I know, you're bugged and I'm about to put my ass in a sling. But the whole matter's been taken out of our jurisdiction. The Feds are running the show now. I think—I don't know for sure—that they moved in a team last night and put you and the lady under surveillance. You try to move and you'll run smack into them."

Briggs's grip on the phone tightened. "Leary let this happen?" He couldn't imagine the ambitious Assistant D.A. stepping aside willingly for anyone.

"He didn't have much choice. I don't know what the Feds have, but it was enough for even Leary. Something very big is going down and you're smack in the middle of it." Sal exhaled softly. "Stay put, buddy, and don't make any waves. Just let 'em bring this one home." His tone was almost pleading, which told Briggs, just in case he hadn't figured it out, exactly how bad things really were.

There were a hundred things he could have said, most of them obscene. But he was past anger now, and into a realm of cold, pure rage. Without another word, he hung up the phone.

"What did he say?" Elsabeth asked, once he'd returned to the bedroom.

"Nothing," Briggs said. He was following the first rule he'd learned the day he hit the streets straight from the academy, never tell civilians anything they didn't need to know.

He went over to the bureau and started pulling clothes out. Swiftly he dressed.

Elsabeth watched him with growing dismay. What had happened to the gentle, passionate man of a short time ago? He seemed to have vanished completely, replaced by a cold, intimidating stranger.

"Where are you going?" she asked, appalled by how weak her voice sounded.

He tucked his shirt into his pants and picked up the gun from the bedside table. "I've got to go out for a while. Stay away from the windows and keep the alarm on. When I get back, I'll knock like this—" He rapped three short, one long on the table. "Don't let anyone else in."

"Briggs, what . . . ?"

"It's nothing. I just need to check some stuff. Just do what I said. And while you're at it, it'd be a good idea to get dressed."

He saw the doubt in her eyes, knew she was struggling to accept what was really not acceptable. He was surprised and grateful when she merely said softly, "All right."

Briggs slipped out the back door and disappeared into the nearby bushes. Elsabeth watched him go from the windows, her stomach churning. She wanted to call after him, to plead with him to be careful, but she knew that any such attempt would only impede him. Clearly he already had enough to deal with.

She threw on her clothes, ran downstairs and checked the bolt on the back door before resetting the alarm. That done, she was at loose ends. Stay away from the windows, he'd said, but the house was filled with windows. That was one of the things she'd liked most about it. The only areas she could think of that didn't have windows were the basement and the attic, and she wasn't much attracted to either. She compromised by deciding it was a good time to clean out the pantry. She was working there, wondering how she'd ended up with no fewer than three jars of sun-dried tomatoes in olive oil, when a sound from outside drew her attention. Johnny and Jacey were in the garden.

Stay away from the windows...keep the alarm on...don't let anyone else in. Oh, God.

She was out the door in an instant, running toward the children.

Briggs moved slowly through the stand of rhododendron bushes that fronted the road. They were the wild variety, standing fully nine feet tall and festooned with large white flowers. Under other circumstances he would have thought them appealing but at the moment they were nothing except camouflage.

He was taking a hell of a chance and he knew it. But he was mad enough for the risk. Scared enough, too. If he'd understood Sal correctly... If he found what he expected to find without first getting his head blown off in the process... If, if, if...

He remembered, suddenly, taking the point in Vietnam, leading his patrol along a jungle path that looked as if it had been carved out only the night before by the endless, infinite enterprise of the enemy. He remembered the silence and the sweat trickling down his back, the ever-present terror that the next instant would be his last. Or worse yet, that he'd live, maimed and helpless like some he had seen.

But that was all in another life, on the other side of the world. This was a pretty country road in the boonies, for God's sake. With any luck at all, he'd find nothing and know that Sal had been wrong.

Far in the back of his mind, he thought of his father. "Luck's a bitch. She'll always let you win a few but when it comes to the big one, she'll forget she ever knew you."

How much he'd despised his father for blaming his own poor judgment and irresponsibility on something that didn't even exist. There was chance and there was fate, and when it was your time to go, you went. Luck had nothing to do with it.

If he had any brains at all, he'd remember that.

Sweat trickled down his back beneath the cotton shirt. An insect buzzed near his ear. He remained motionless, making no attempt to swat it away. The bushes completely concealed him but he could see clearly down most of the length of the road. A car was coming, driving slowly. He stiffened and the hand holding the gun tightened.

The car was a four-door sedan, dark gray, with all of the windows rolled down to admit the breeze. A man and a woman were seated in the front, the man driving. They were laughing together. The woman said something, her expression and the gesture she made suggesting she was commenting on the beauty of the day. The man smiled and nodded. They drove on.

Briggs eased his grip on the gun slightly. Sightseers out for a pleasant drive with no idea of what they might have walked into. He envied innocence like that. When he really tried, he could even remember what it felt like.

He moved on, all his senses painfully alert. Near the turn in the road he crouched down, waiting. It didn't take as long as he'd expected. Watching the foliage on the other side of the road, he saw first motion then the slight irregularity of color that indicated something— someone—was standing behind the branches.

Briggs smiled grimly. One, possibly two. He moved on, retracing his steps toward the house. All total, he counted four guard posts and thought there might be more. It was all the confirmation he needed. Sal was right, somebody had just upped the ante on what had already been a very dangerous game. Somebody who had no scruples about using an innocent woman as bait.

He recalled the worm on the hook and thanked God that Elsabeth didn't know.

Johnny and Jacey looked bewildered. They didn't understand what she was saying. "I'm always glad to see you," Elsabeth told them. "But it would be a good idea for you to go home right now."

She was kneeling in front of them, looking them both in the eye to give urgency to what she was saying, trying not to frighten them.

Jacey stared back at her. Her child's gaze was clear and candid, unfettered by deception. "What's the matter?"

"Nothing," Elsabeth said too quickly. "It's just that I'm . . . working. Besides, isn't your dad on vacation this week? He and your mom probably have something planned for you all to do."

"Daddy's taking a nap," Jacey said evenly. "Mommy's painting the bathroom. She told us to go out and play."

Silently Elsabeth cursed. She couldn't explain the fear pounding at her but she knew she had to get the children out of there as quickly as possible.

"I'm sorry," she said softly, "I have to work."

"You're doing magic, aren't you?" Johnny asked.

"You know that's what I am, a magician."

"Real magic," he explained, spelling it out with his child's firmness.

Oh, if only she could. If only she could wave her hand and make them all disappear, or make whatever the danger was go away. Make Briggs come back and erase the grim look from his face, make everything all right again.

Not that it had been ever since Dickinson. She couldn't forget that he was dead, couldn't let herself forget, because then who knew what would happen.

"You have to go home," she said, not so gently now. Better they should be frightened than anything worse.

"Why?" Johnny asked. He was one of those children who always needed a reason, a trait she happened to admire but which at the moment was horribly inconvenient.

"Because I said so," she tried, doing her best to sound like their mother whom she knew a little. Young Mrs. Cavendish had what Elsabeth always thought of as "the voice," that special tone of absolute, unswervable authority.

They hesitated, bewildered by behavior that had no precedent in their experience. But she was their friend and they didn't want her to be unhappy.

"All right," Jacey said. They looked at her a moment longer before scampering back through the bushes and across the road.

Elsabeth stood up slowly. She watched until they were out of sight. Only then did she become aware of the shrill beeping behind her. The security alarm had gone off.

Out on the road Briggs heard it. He sprinted, head down, running for everything he was worth. The yard was empty, there was no sight of anyone, no sound... The beeping stopped. He burst into the kitchen in time to see Elsabeth punching the last button into the control panel beside the back door.

"Oh, geez," he said, slumping over, his hands on his knees with the gun still dangling. "Don't do this to me."

She saw the fear in him and it strengthened her own calmness. "Jacey and Johnny were outside. I didn't think about the alarm."

She knew. Somehow, she had figured it out, or at least part of it. Briggs sighed deeply. He shut the door and slipped the gun back into the holster. Quietly he said, "Why don't you fix us some coffee?"

He half expected her to argue but she didn't say a word. Briggs sat down at the table and watched her as she filled the pot. She looked gorgeous, as always, and scared, and determined. He was going to have his work cut out for him.

When the coffee was ready, she brought two cups over to the table. "All right," she said, "now tell me what's going on." He was about to answer when she added, "And don't you dare say nothing or I swear I'll make you sorry you ever set foot outside the big city. Something big is obviously happening and I have a right to know what it is.''

He couldn't argue with her, at least not while she was holding the mugs of steaming coffee directly over his lap. The lady had style, he had to give her that.

"Sit down," he said quietly.

She did as he said. In return, he told her, at least as much as he thought she had to know.

Elsabeth listened carefully before shaking her head. "I don't believe it. I know Alphonse. He's a good man with a wife and children. I can't believe he'd betray me like that."

"If he's got a wife and kids, he's got expenses," Briggs said patiently. "Dangle enough money and just about anybody will bite."

Elsabeth frowned, still unconvinced. But rather than pursue the point, she tried a different tack. "Is that why you went out, to see if there was any sign of trouble?"

"Not exactly," Briggs hedged. "It seems Sal isn't the only one to know about Alphonse. We've got company."

"I don't understand."

"There's a dozen or so guys with automatic weapons hiding in the bushes up and down the road. I spotted them and they probably spotted me, so for the moment, we're even."

"That's good news, isn't it?"

"Not exactly." He paused, choosing his words carefully. He still couldn't bring himself to tell her all he suspected, but he was going to have to come close.

"I know how this works," he said. "I've been there. They'll have convinced themselves that they can protect you."

"But you don't agree?"

Briggs took a sip of his coffee before he looked at her directly. "We'll have to wait until dark, then we go."

Elsabeth put down her cup. She understood what he was saying, she just wished she didn't.

"Let me get this straight. You don't think those men out there can protect us but you also believe they'd try to stop us from leaving. Aren't they police like you?"

"Not exactly." He ignored her surprise and went on hastily. "Most of them won't really know the situation. I'd rather not rely on them."

Elsabeth considered that. The explanation was hardly clear but she sensed it was all she was going to get from him at the moment. That should have bothered her and would have if she hadn't been so completely, deep-down-inside convinced that Briggs wouldn't let any harm come to her. For a woman who had always prided herself on self-sufficiency, it was a shock to realize how much she was willing to depend on him. But then life was like that, filled with curveballs you couldn't outrun or hope to duck. That was what made it so interesting.

"Go where?" she asked.

"I've got a cabin in Maine. I use it for writing. We'll go there."

"How?" she persisted. "How will we get there?"

"By car. That's the quickest and safest way."

"But they know the car you drive and they certainly know mine."

He'd forgotten that she made a living figuring out the cleverest paths to subterfuge. She'd know, without his having to tell her, how complicated escape would be.

"I've got another car," he said. "It's garaged not too far from here. The department doesn't know about it."

The extra car, the battered old M.G. convertible for which he had unabashed fondness, was a holdover from his days on drug detail. Back then it had been drummed into his head that you always had a way out, a back-door escape from any situation. He'd acquired the car because he liked it but he'd kept knowledge of it from the department for reasons he'd never cared to examine before.

"Won't that get you into trouble?" Elsabeth asked. "Helping me get out of here?"

"Let me worry about that."

"Which means yes, doesn't it, even though you don't want to admit it? I've got to tell you, Briggs, the strong, silent type wears thin awfully quick."

He looked at her in surprise. "What do you mean?"

"I mean that the last time I checked I was an independent, fully functional human being in charge of her own life and beholden to no one except maybe Great-aunt Georgette who, let me tell you, had her own opinions about men trying to cosset women and protect them from unpleasant truths."

"Cosset?" It was such a delightfully old-fashioned word that he couldn't help but grin. "All I'm trying to do is keep you from getting your head shot off. This is the big leagues, sweetheart. Those guys outside play for keeps."

"About them, who exactly are they?"

He answered reluctantly. "Federal agents, and no—before you ask—Sal didn't say why they'd been brought in." Briggs had his own ideas but he wasn't about to share them, not right then, anyway.

"Somebody sitting behind a desk in Washington made the decision to get involved," he went on. "Now maybe you want to believe that person is smart enough and experienced enough to decide what happens to you, but I'm not so sure. I know he—whoever he is—could have done it because he's trying to advance his career, or because he's fed up with his wife and women in general, or because he was hung over this morning or his ulcer's acting up or whatever. There could be a hundred reasons and maybe only one or two of them are right. The fact is your life is on the line and I am not comfortable with that."

"I'm not too happy about it myself," Elsabeth murmured. She had actually thought this man had a romantic side to him? He was as hard-nosed a cynic as she had ever encountered. Worse yet, she suspected he was right.

"Then we go," Briggs said. "As soon as it's dark."

Elsabeth glanced out the window at the bright morning sun. She sighed inwardly. It was going to be another long day. Trying to put the best twist on it that she could, she smiled faintly. "I'm not much good at running, Briggs. You'll have to teach me how."

He didn't tell her that he wasn't much good at it himself. He suspected she already knew.

Chapter 10

They passed the day as best they could. Elsabeth went through her practice routine, trying her best not to notice Briggs sitting at the kitchen table, breaking down his gun. He took it completely apart, and cleaned and oiled each piece before reassembling it. She said nothing about that but the sight was chilling. They watched a little television before turning again to chess. This time they managed to play a game all the way through. Briggs provided stiff competition but Elsabeth managed to pull out in the end, checkmating his king. He took the defeat good-naturedly, then beat her solidly in the rematch.

Toward twilight Briggs went out to check his car. He did it casually, conscious of the eyes watching him. The keys were in his palm. He slipped them into the ignition and left the driver's side door slightly ajar, not enough to be noticeable or to run down the battery but sufficient to give them the second or two they might need.

When he came back into the kitchen Elsabeth was getting an old wicker picnic basket out of the pantry.

"What's that for?" Briggs asked.

"It's Zared's carrier."

"Uh . . . you're not thinking . . ."

"Well, of course I am. You don't seriously suggest he should stay here by himself?"

"I thought cats were supposed to be self-sufficient."

"Maybe they are but Zared doesn't know that. Besides, he likes to travel."

"Great," Briggs muttered under his breath. It wasn't enough to be on the run, he also had to take a meat loaf masquerading as a cat along with him.

"It'll be dark soon," he said, trying hard not to notice how lovely she looked in the simple jeans and T-shirt she'd put on. "Let's get some rest."

They settled on the couch. With the blinds drawn and the lights off, the room was filled with shadows. Elsabeth shut her eyes to escape them and sighed softly.

Briggs hesitated only a moment before he put his arm around her and drew her close. After the incendiary night they had shared, he'd resolved not to touch her again until this whole sorry business was over and done with. But then he'd resolved a whole lot of things in his life—to learn French, see Antarctica, take up hang gliding, and a couple of hundred more things. He'd even accomplished a few of them. But not this one.

Elsabeth stiffened slightly before letting herself relax. She was so damn tired and scared, and tired of being scared. His warmth and strength, the solid nearness of him, all felt so good. She folded her legs up on the couch and snuggled closer. He put both arms around her and let his cheek rest against the top of her head.

"It's okay," he murmured gently. "We're going to come out of this just fine."

"You bet," she said, praying it was true. She had never realized before how long the summer light lingered. The waiting was painful but there was no alternative.

Around 10:00 p.m. Briggs suggested she go upstairs, use the bathroom and turn on her bedroom light. He did the same downstairs. An hour later they turned both lights off. The house was very still. Zared was in his carrier and being unexpectedly tolerant of it. Briggs and Elsabeth were both ready. She waited on the couch while he went once more to look carefully out of the window.

"No moon tonight," he said quietly. "That's a break." He let the slat of the blind fall back into place and walked toward the door. "Let's go."

Elsabeth took a deep breath. She stood up but didn't move. "Briggs, are you absolutely sure you want to do this?"

He frowned, his silvered eyes staring through her, gauging the level of her resistance. "The situation hasn't changed any in the last few hours. I don't see there's any alternative."

"Aren't your superiors going to be very upset at you, not to mention the federal authorities?"

"Probably."

"You're so close to retirement. It just doesn't seem right."

He came away from the door and took a step toward her, his face grim. "I'm a senior police officer with twenty years experience. Part of what I'm paid for is to exercise my own judgment. Anybody who's got a problem with that knows what they can do with it. Now let's go."

His eyes held her until, reluctantly, she nodded.

Briggs's hand was on the doorknob when he froze. "Don't move," he said tersely. From the other side of the house, near the back door, came a faint sound.

His pistol was out, in his hand and ready. He pushed Elsabeth behind the settee near the door and crouched down beside her. Again they heard the sound.

"It's the raccoons," she whispered, "or the wind."

He motioned her to be quiet. Heart-straining moments passed before the back door creaked open. Elsabeth had known fear in her life, quite a bit of it in the last few days, but she had never experienced anything like the bone-chilling terror that rushed through her now. Her legs went limp and she knew that if she hadn't already been kneeling, she would have fallen.

Could the men outside have decided to enter the house? But why? And surely they knew Briggs was there and would be armed. They wouldn't take such a risk.

But others would.

There were two of them. She could see that much through the dim shadows. They were both large and she guessed they could be the same two men from the parking lot. The men who had killed Dickinson come to finish the job.

They entered the kitchen cautiously. Both carried rifles. They were dressed in black and wore black hoods over their heads, concealing their faces. Beside her, she felt Briggs begin to move.

Her hand lashed out, tightening on his broad wrist. Silently, with her eyes, she entreated him to be still, do nothing, trust her. With her other hand, she tried to pantomime what would happen but she could see that he didn't understand.

One of the men had reached the staircase. The other was still in the kitchen. He had reached the center of the braided oval rug that covered most of the floor. That was the best she could hope for. Just as Briggs reached down to remove her hand she reached out and lightly touched the carving on the side of the fireplace mantle. There was a low, grinding sound. A hole opened in the kitchen floor. The man cried out and flailed with his arms but his weight pushed the rug down into the hole and him with it. Both fell, vanishing from sight.

The second man whirled around but before he could take a step, Briggs launched himself at him, bringing him down with a heavy thud. As the two grappled, the room was suddenly flooded with light. Other men, at least half a dozen, pushed through the back door.

"FBI," one of them yelled. *"Everybody freeze."*

Briggs was too busy keeping the assailant from firing his automatic weapon to listen. The officers hesitated, uncertain of who was who and not anxious to get in the middle. With a massive effort that took almost all his strength, Briggs drove his knee into the man's midsection and at the same time wrested the weapon away. It went skittering across the floor and came to rest against the fireplace.

One of the officers shoved the muzzle of his gun close to Briggs's face while another did the same to the other man. The assailant knew when he was beaten. He crouched, panting on the ground, and offered no resistance. Briggs wasn't so cooperative. He was tired, fed up, hurting and flat out of anything resembling patience. Angrily he shoved the gun aside and got to his feet.

"Who's in charge?" Briggs demanded in a low, deadly tone that brooked no challenge.

One of the men stepped forward. He was tall, well-built and armed. His eyes were steel cold but they wavered slightly as they met Briggs's.

"Stevens, FBI," he said. "You're Caldwell?"

Briggs nodded. He came up close to the other man, ignoring the gun. "FBI? Is that right? They must have been having a real bad day when they took you on board. How long were you planning to wait in the bushes, Stevens? Until you were sure they'd had plenty of time to surprise us? Until you had two counts of murder one to pin on them?"

The agent's face was bright red, his mouth twisted. "You were never in that kind of danger," he claimed. "We were right behind them."

Briggs muttered something that made it clear what he thought of that. Stevens stiffened. His look became even more defensive—and belligerent. Elsabeth didn't wait to see how he would respond. Quickly she stepped between them.

"The other man is down there," she said, pointing to the hole in the kitchen floor. "Shouldn't somebody check on him?"

"He's out cold, lady," one of the others offered, clearly as anxious as she was to defuse the confrontation. "What the hell happened there, anyway?"

"He fell through a trapdoor," Elsabeth said. She took Briggs's arm and tugged gently, drawing him away. He came reluctantly, his breathing labored. Never in his life had he been so angry. The intensity of his own rage shocked him into stillness. For a moment, standing in front of Stevens, he could have done anything. *Anything.*

"Georgette told me about this one along with the others," Elsabeth was saying. "She showed me how to activate it but I never actually tried to before this. I'm amazed it worked. Very glad, too, of course." She rattled on, not sure how much of what she was saying made sense and not caring. Nothing mattered except soothing the blind, murderous anger she had felt coming from Briggs. Thank God, he was a strong man. Almost anyone else would have snapped. She'd come close to it herself and she only half understood what had happened. Briggs understood it all, she knew that. In time he'd tell her. She'd make sure of it. But for the moment nothing mattered except calming him.

With him beside her, she looked down into the darkness beneath the kitchen. "That part of the cellar is sealed off from the rest. I asked Georgette why, but she said she didn't know."

"We'll have to get him out," one of the officers said. He looked at Briggs cautiously. "A couple of us'll go down."

"I'll go," Briggs said quietly. He glanced around at the other men and pointed to one. "With you."

Nobody argued. In the aftermath of the raid, they were all uneasy about the plan they had followed. It had seemed right at the time, considering the stakes. But face-to-face with the two people who had been used as bait and could have been killed, second thoughts abounded.

A flashlight was shone into the hole as Briggs and the other man lowered themselves. The dirt floor was a good eight feet below. Deeper than any root cellar, Briggs thought. Deeper even than the rest of the basement where it was almost impossible to stand upright. He had no difficulty doing so here.

Bending down beside the unconscious man, he pulled the black hood off. The blunt features were slack but clearly recognizable. Charlie Gingrich, alias the Chumpster, had been caught.

Together, Briggs and the agent lifted Gingrich enough to get a rope around his waist. The other end of the rope was thrown up to the agents waiting above. Cursing and sweating, they hauled the inert hit man out of the basement.

Briggs slipped the safety back on the automatic rifle Gingrich had been carrying, offering silent thanks that it hadn't gone off. The rug was rolled up and pushed through the hole, and the agent climbed out. It was Briggs's turn next but he delayed long enough to look around. There was a small, roughly hewn bench in one corner beside what looked like a pile of rags. He bent over to examine them and frowned in surprise.

"Briggs?" Elsabeth called from above. "Are you coming out?"

"In a minute. Come down here and take a look at this."

Two of the agents were repairing the wires the assailants had cut to silence the alarm system. The others were securing the two men in separate cars that had been brought up outside. Gingerly Elsabeth lowered herself into the hole.

"What is it?" she asked.

"My guess is an old mattress, and look here." He held up a moldy length of cloth. "What's left of a blanket."

A chill ran through Elsabeth that had only partly to do with the damp dankness of the hidden cellar. "Why would anyone want to sleep down here?"

"Maybe they didn't want to," Briggs suggested. "Maybe they didn't have any choice."

"You can't mean somebody forced them..."

Briggs had turned away from her, following a glint of metal exposed by the beam of the flashlight. "What's that?"

Elsabeth wrapped her arms around herself. "A box."

"Let's take it up with us."

That was fine with her so long as they got out of there. Events were catching up with her. Her head spun and her throat was painfully dry.

She climbed up the rope first with Briggs's help, then waited while he emerged. Together, they closed the trapdoor and replaced the rug over it. Stevens came back as they were finishing.

"We're going," he said shortly. He looked at Elsabeth. "The lady's already identified the other intruder as Dan Ruglio. We picked up Mick MacMann earlier today, so that's a clean sweep. I'll need a statement from you both but it can wait until morning."

"How many men are you leaving?" Briggs demanded.

"Two, they'll be outside, but I really don't think you have anything more to be concerned about. These guys were strictly small-timers who screwed up. Our information is that their problem with Dickinson was personal. He'd caught them skimming betting receipts. So there's no reason to think your witness is in any further danger."

He looked hard at Briggs. "I know you don't like what we did, Caldwell, but it worked. Gingrich and the others are mob connected. Given what we've got on them now, they'll be singing like birds. They're the only ones who have to worry about protection. Miss Grace is off the hook."

Briggs did not reply. After a moment Stevens left. The door banged shut behind him.

"Is it really over?" Elsabeth asked when they were alone. She had let Zared out of the carrier. He stalked off, tail high, making it clear he wanted nothing to do with humans for a while.

Briggs shrugged. "Stevens sure made it sound that way." He smiled suddenly, his eyes warm and gentle on her. "I could use some coffee. How about you?"

"I guess. Sleep seems pretty impossible. Besides," she added, remembering the box, "I would like to see what's in there."

She made the coffee and added generous slices of lemon pound cake to the tray. While she was at it, she also filled a thermos and put slices of the cake in a basket.

"Would you take this to the men outside?" she asked.

Briggs did and returned with their thanks. The coffee was appreciated but the gesture even more so.

"You don't think much of Stevens, do you?" Elsabeth asked as she set the tray on the low table in front of the couch.

"No, I don't, but let's not talk about that now. The box is locked. Do you have a hairpin?"

Elsabeth had to search for one, all the while teasing Briggs that he didn't have some more sophisticated means at his disposal. He did but it was good to see her smile. He straightened the hairpin, hooked it slightly at one end, and probed gently at the old, rust-bound lock. It proved more stubborn than he'd expected but after a few minutes' effort, it opened.

Inside was a small, leather-bound book.

Briggs moved to pick it up but Elsabeth stopped him. "Wait. It's very old. We have to be careful."

Slowly she slipped both hands into the box and moved them under the book. With great caution, she lifted it and laid it on the table before them. The binding creaked as she opened it and a soft fluttering of dust rose from the pages that still remained firm.

"Can you make out the writing?" Briggs asked.

"It's difficult . . ." She bent closer, struggling to decipher the pale, spider-thin script that bisected the first page. "Byrnes . . . 'Martha Elizabeth Byrnes, Her Book.' That's what it says. Byrnes is a very old name around here. There's a Byrnes Road nearby and on the other side of town there's a Byrnes Lane.'' She thought for a moment, remembering references Georgette had let drop over the years. ''I'm not sure but I think the Byrnes family may have owned this house, or at least the part of it that's original.''

''How long ago would that have been?''

''Early 1700s when the town was first settled.'' She looked up excitedly. ''Briggs, this book could be more than two hundred and fifty years old. That's incredible. Whatever's in it, it's an important historical document.''

He smiled, glad that something had taken her mind off far more recent events. Not that he didn't share her pleasure. The writer in him was awestruck at the thought that anyone's words would endure so long. Envious, too, of the flax-based paper and the nonacidic ink that allowed such works to survive centuries when modern books were yellowed and crumbling after only a few decades.

''What did Martha Byrnes have to say for herself?'' he asked.

Elsabeth turned the page with great care. Slowly she read the fragile script. ''Let's see, 'April the Third'— no year given—'planted beans and potatoes, also thyme. Sent to Cousin Daniel in Fairfield for six of his apple saplings. The orchard does well.''' She turned another page. '''May the Fifteenth—peas in, also marrows and the small pumpkins. The daffodils have bloomed in the north pasture. Rain yesterday.'''

''It's a gardening book,'' Briggs said, his interest beginning to wane. ''She recorded what she planted. Don't gardeners still do that?''

Elsabeth nodded. "But there's more. She's included recipes." Her voice trailed off. "Hmm, that's odd."

"What is?"

"Nothing, it just doesn't sound as though it would taste very good. Maybe it's medicinal. What's this? 'Visitors tonight, four traveling south from Massachusetts colony. The eldest is weary but they would not agree to stay more than a day. The danger is still too great. Surely they are wrong. There have never been burnings here and never in the colonies in my lifetime. And yet the terror remains.'"

"What danger, what burnings?" Briggs asked.

"I don't know. She could mean Indians, but this area was settled peacefully."

"She says there weren't any burnings here."

"Yet they were still afraid." Puzzled, Elsabeth looked through several more pages. "Look, there are other references to 'visitors.' She never mentions their names and they always pass on quickly. Don't you think that's odd?"

"Maybe they were smugglers?" Briggs suggested. "That would explain the trapdoors and the hidden basement. Smugglers would need a quick getaway or a secure place to hide."

"Nobody ever burned smugglers," Elsabeth said. "The worst that ever happened to them was that they were hanged. The only people who were burned were witches…" She inhaled sharply as her eyes went dark.

Briggs shot her a quick look. "You're not serious? Witches?"

"It sounds crazy, but—" Her mind was racing, trying to come to terms with what seemed at first glance to be inconceivable. She had never heard of suspected witches being hidden, and yet she had to admit it made sense. "If this book does date from the early days of Redding, if would have been about 1725. The Salem witch trials were thirty-three years before then, but still within the lifetimes of at least some of the people living here. Witches were burned in England in 1712 and in Scotland as late as 1727. The horror of that—and the fear—would have been very real."

Briggs looked from the book to Elsabeth and back again. "How do you know all that?" he asked quietly.

"Georgette told me. She was interested in the history of witchcraft and the persecutions. She—"

"Why didn't she find the book?"

"I don't know. Maybe she never went down in that part of the basement."

"But she knew how the trapdoor worked, she showed you. Don't tell me she lived how many years in this house—several decades—and never took a look down there?"

"It does seem odd," Elsabeth admitted.

He shook his head, amused by the notion that had just occurred to him. "I think she left it as a surprise for you. Maybe she thought you'd glean some magic from it."

"Magic doesn't have anything to do with witchcraft," Elsabeth said. "Witchcraft—real witchcraft, not the sick Satanism some people indulge in—was a religion. It still is to some people. Magic is . . ."

"Trickery?"

"Yes, in part. It has to do with making things seem other than what they are, transforming them into what we'd like them to be."

"You don't think the old practitioners of witch-craft tried to do that?"

"Maybe . . . I don't know. But if that is what Martha Byrnes is talking about here, then witchcraft still existed in the colonies long after Salem. Could there have been other houses like this, safe houses between one colony and another?"

"There was an underground railroad for slaves," Briggs reminded her. "Why not for people who were persecuted because of their religion?"

"If that's true, it opens the way for a whole new historical study of the colonies."

Briggs nodded politely but he was far more interested in the way the light glinted off her red-gold hair. The powerful surge of adrenaline that had coursed through his body during the attack was beginning to ebb. In its aftermath he was almost too relaxed. He knew that he had to stay alert, he didn't trust Stevens or anything the federal agent said. The whole story about Dickinson and the three killers smelled. If the accountant had caught them skimming, he would have told his own higher-ups immediately. Chumpster and the others would have been taken care of before they'd had a clue what was happening.

He was still tempted to stick to his original plan: get Elsabeth in the car and hightail it for Maine. But it would take time for whoever was behind the attack to regroup, time Briggs could use to find out what was really going on.

Elsabeth was absorbed in the book. He was glad to see that. Let her wonder about long-ago witches and things that went bump in the night. He'd deal with the here and now.

Much later, after Elsabeth had drifted to sleep in his arms, the book forgotten in her lap, he carried her to bed. For a moment he considered leaving her alone but decided against it. He couldn't afford the distraction of making love to her again no matter how much his body ached for hers. But he could hold her close and safe through what was left of the night.

Too soon day would come and with it the renewal of danger. He had plans to make. Stretched out on the bed, he touched his lips gently to her forehead and thought about how precious she had become to him in such a short time.

And how he would deal with anyone foolish enough to try to take her from him.

Chapter 11

Stevens was waiting for them when they got to police headquarters the next morning to give their statements. Leary was also there. The Assistant District Attorney was obviously unhappy. He paced up and down, chewing gum fiercely, glaring at them when a secretary showed them into his office.

"Come on, come on," he said. "Let's get this over with."

Stevens appeared equally eager to get on to other things. "There's not much they've got to add," he said, speaking not to them but to Leary. The senior agent seemed to be repeating a point that had already been discussed between the two.

"You're sure about that?" Briggs asked. He spoke pleasantly, as though everything was indeed a mere matter of routine. But they weren't fooled and neither was Elsabeth. She had awakened alone in the bed but with the imprint of his body beside her. An imprint that seemed to carry a lingering sense of anger so profound that, even now, she could hardly bear to contemplate it. If the passion of their lovemaking hadn't so perfectly attuned her to his feelings, she would have thought her imagination was running away with her. As it was, she knew something very bad was happening.

"Sit down, Miss Grace," Leary said, pulling out a chair for her. He propped himself on the edge of the table and smiled. "We'll have you out of here in no time." Looking at Briggs, he added, "We'll take your statement separately, Detective. A stenographer is waiting next door."

Elsabeth thought he would argue but instead Briggs merely shrugged. "Okay. Like you said, this shouldn't take long."

Leary frowned, surprised at his easy compliance. "When you're done," he said, "D'Angelo wants to see you."

Briggs nodded. He met Elsabeth's puzzled gaze, smiled reassuringly, and was gone.

With his departure the mood in the room changed. Stevens visibly relaxed. "Okay," he said, "let's wrap this up."

"Just describe what happened at your residence last night," Leary instructed. "The stenographer will take it all down." He nodded toward the nondescript man sitting in a corner. "You'll sign a transcript and that will be that." He glanced at Stevens. "Okay?"

The agent nodded. "Fine."

"Then I'll be going," Leary said, obviously relieved. "I've got a meeting. Nice to have seen you again, Miss Grace."

He flashed her another vacant smile and vanished out the door.

"Pretty good trick," Elsabeth muttered under her breath.

"What's that?" Stevens asked, looking at her impatiently.

"Disappearing people," she said. "First Briggs, then Leary. If I read you right, I'll be next. One minute I'm the sole witness in a mob killing and the next minute everything's coming up roses. Amazing."

"That's how we work, Miss Grace. Now if you don't mind—" He took a seat opposite her and gestured to the stenographer that they were ready to begin. "Just the facts, please. There's no need for a lot of detail."

Elsabeth got the message. She kept it short and sweet. The sooner she got out of there, the better she'd like it.

Briggs felt the same way. He left the interviewing room, ignored the door immediately next to it where he was supposed to go, and instead stalked down the corridor in search of Sal. He found him in the squad room, sipping morosely from a plastic cup of coffee that looked to be at least a couple of days old.

"How can you drink that garbage?" he said by way of greeting.

Sal looked surprised. "What garbage? This is the same stuff you drink."

"Not anymore." He took Sal's arm and led him into an empty corner where they couldn't be overheard. "Let's have it."

The lieutenant sighed. He was a big man, soft around the middle with the look of an aging hound dog. Life had a way of living down to his expectations yet he managed to stay hopeful. Or at least he always had.

He slumped in a battered chair and said, "Did I ever tell you my mother wanted me to go into the grocery business? My uncle Dominic had a nice little store two blocks down from where we lived. He offered to take me in, but no, I had to go to the academy. Had to be a cop. Really smart."

"You would have gone nuts standing behind a counter," Briggs said. "Besides, you're not just a cop, you're a damn good one. That has to count for something."

"I used to think so," Sal said. "Lately I'm not so sure."

He looked at Briggs for a long moment before abruptly jerking his head in the direction of his office. "Come on."

Briggs followed him with a growing sense of unease. Sal's rank entitled him to a private office but he hardly ever used it. He preferred to be out in the squad room with his men. The office got used only in the worst situations.

The walls of the office were glass covered by blinds, which Sal kept drawn. The desk was bare, testifying to how rarely he sat at it. Binders of official documents overflowed rickety metal shelves. A sickly philodendron monopolized the thin rays of sun coming through windows in need of cleaning.

Sal plunked down in the swivel chair, took a ring of keys from his pants pocket, and inserted one into the lock on the top drawer. He removed a blue-jacketed file and dumped it on the desk.

"Your papers came through this morning."

Briggs looked from the blue file to Sal and back again. "What're you talking about? They're not due for another month."

"Chalk it up to the efficiency of the department."

"That's bull."

Sal shrugged. "You were eligible for retirement, you requested same, your papers have come through. So what if they're a little early?"

"You know damn well what. This thing with Elsa-beth—"

"Is signed, sealed and delivered, at least according to Leary. I have it on good authority from downstairs that he put in a call to the powers that be. Said the Grace case was your last and there was no sense making you hang around now that it's over. Presto, you're out. Full pension, all benefits, a month early. Most guys would be dancing in the halls. By the way, I'm supposed to collect your badge and gun before you leave the building."

Briggs muttered something low and virulent.

"What was that?" Sal inquired mildly.

"You know damn well. This whole thing smells. It has from the beginning. I trust Leary about as much as I'd trust a three-card monte player with a brace of aces up his sleeve. As for Stevens—"

"Never mind, I get the picture. Question is, do you? You're out officially—at your own request—and you can bet Leary will make sure everyone knows it. If you refuse to go along, if you walk out of this building still armed and with your badge, you'll be breaking the law. Leary'll say you've gone renegade, maybe even suggest you're somehow mixed up in Dickinson's murder. You'll get hauled up on charges, at the least. You could end up facing some buckaroo Fed who isn't too picky about who he shoots."

Sal shook his head sadly. "You can't fight city hall or whoever the hell Leary's working for these days."

"I can't *not* fight, either. Elsabeth—" He broke off, unwilling to expose his feelings and not sure what he'd say, anyway. One thing was for sure, she had him tied up in knots. The funny part was that he actually liked it.

Sal nodded sympathetically. "Yeah, it's tough." He waited, not speaking, giving Briggs time.

He didn't need much. All his life he'd worked hard at coming to terms with reality. In the process he'd gotten to know it pretty well. Life—real life—was capricious, unrelenting and sometimes plain rotten. His grandmother—tough, hard-drinking old woman that she'd been—had summed it up neatly. "Life's one damn thing after another and then you die." With words of wisdom like those echoing in his ears, was it any wonder he was hard-nosed?

He put his gun on the desk. From the inner pocket of his jacket, he took the plain leather billfold that held his badge. For a moment he held it cupped in his hand, looking at the symbol of his identity for so many years. Softly he laid it, too, in front of Sal.

"I guess that's it," Briggs said, "except for these."
On an afterthought he added the keys to the department car he used. There was no point in trying to hold
onto them. The vehicle could be too easily recognized.

"Yeah," Sal said, locking the gun, the badge, and
the keys in the desk drawer. He stood up. "So what's
the plan?"

Briggs raised an eyebrow. "Plan?"

"You still got the cabin in Maine?"

"Maybe."

"I never heard of it. Here." He handed over a key
he had removed from his own key ring.

"What's this?"

"It's the spare to my locker downstairs. You might
see something you like." He lifted his shoulders. "For
old time's sake."

Briggs was surprised and a little alarmed. Sal had
always played pretty much by the book, unlike some
other guys he knew. The lieutenant's outrage at what
had been done to one of his men wouldn't have been
enough by itself to make him break the patterns of a
lifetime. He had to believe something very bad was
going down.

Briggs wished he could believe he was wrong but he
knew better. All his instincts were working overtime
and the message he was getting wasn't good.

"Thanks," he said shortly.

Sal nodded. "Keep in touch." He looked hard at
him as he said that, making the message clear. Sal
would be at the other end of the phone if Briggs
needed him.

Which was nice to know, and might even come in handy, but at the moment nothing much counted except getting Elsabeth and getting out.

But when he got back to the interviewing room, it was empty. Leary was gone and so was Stevens. Of Elsabeth, there was no sign at all.

Briggs didn't hesitate. He barreled down the hallway, scattering people out of his way. He slammed open the door to Leary's office and pushed past the secretary who babbled something at him about needing an appointment. Leary was at his desk. He jumped up when he saw Briggs and looked around frantically for some way out. There wasn't any.

"Where is she?" Briggs snarled. He picked Leary up bodily, and holding him a foot off the ground, slammed him hard into the wall.

The Assistant D.A.'s face convulsed with fear. *"You're crazy! I'll have you broken for this! You'll—"*

"I'm very angry, Mr. Leary," Briggs said slowly. His face was close to the other man's. He spoke distinctly, shaping each word with care so there wouldn't be any misunderstanding. "I am almost out of patience. That is not a good thing for me to be. Now you tell me real fast, where is she?"

"Ladies' room," Leary croaked. "Last I saw of her, she was going into the ladies' room. Let me down, for God's sake, I can't breathe."

Briggs dropped him. He landed with a thud, red-faced and gasping.

"I'll break you, Caldwell! I swear you'll regret the day you—"

Briggs didn't hear him. He blasted through the outer office, ignored the cowering secretary and headed straight down the hall. The ladies' room was halfway to the elevators on the left side. He pushed open the door without hesitation. Three women were standing in front of a row of sinks. One of them was Elsabeth.

She stared at him disbelievingly. *"Briggs..."*

"Let's go," he said.

"This is the ladies' room."

"I know that, let's go."

"But you're not supposed to...that is, you're..."

He took hold of her arm and led her back into the hallway. "Yeah, I know. It's okay. I just wasn't sure where you were, that's all. I got a little concerned."

He punched the button for the elevator, decided it was taking too long, and led her over to the stairs.

"Where are we going?" Elsabeth demanded. She was just getting her poise back after having been rattled by the sight of a large, overbearing male trespassing in what was probably the last sacrosanct female place on earth—labor and delivery rooms having long since been dropped off the list and even kitchens being regularly violated.

"The basement," he said as though that ought to be all the explanation she needed. It wasn't.

"I'm going home," she said, trying without much success to dig her heels into the peeling linoleum.

He dismissed the notion as unworthy of a reply. At the bottom of the steps was a long hallway that ended in a gunmetal-gray door covered with uncounted coats of paint. Stenciled across it in red was Men's Locker Room.

"This is getting to be a habit," Elsabeth muttered as he pushed the door open and went in, still keeping a firm hold on her. "I'll wait outside," she offered.

He shook his head firmly. "You're not getting out of my sight. Besides, this won't take long."

Elsabeth glanced nervously along the rows of lockers fronted by narrow benches. Through a separate door she could see a white-tiled shower area. Fortunately it and the locker room both seemed empty.

Briggs stopped at the end of one of the rows. A small label on the front of the locker read D'Angelo. He took a key from his pocket and inserted it in the lock. The door slid open. Inside was a fresh shirt, a spare tie, a shaving kit, a couple of books and a shoe box. Inside the shoe box was a pistol and a box of shells. Briggs put the pistol in his usual spot at the small of his back. The shells went into his pocket. He replaced the box and shut the door, making sure it was locked. His own locker was further down the row. Strictly speaking, he should empty it. But that could wait. There was nothing especially important in it and there were more pressing matters to be considered. Staying alive, for instance.

"Okay, let's go," he said.

Elsabeth looked at the name on the locker, confirming to herself that she'd read it right. "You're going to explain all this. You know that, don't you?"

He nodded. "Later."

They left the building by a back door that gave way onto an alley. At the end of the alley farthest from the street, a narrow passage stretched between old, ramshackle buildings pressed close together. They followed it for most of a block, emerging, finally, far from the police station.

"What was all that about?" Elsabeth demanded. They stood in front of a fruit-and-vegetable store waiting as a city bus approached.

"I got a little upset at Leary," Briggs said. "Odds are he's looking for us."

"And the gun? It belongs to Lieutenant D'Angelo, doesn't it? How did you get the key to his locker?"

"He gave it to me while he was collecting my gun and badge."

Elsabeth's eyes widened. "What are you talking about?"

The bus arrived, exhaling great bursts of diesel fumes. Briggs waited until they were on board before he answered. When they were seated toward the back, far removed from the few other passengers, he said, "Remember I told you that I'd put in my papers?"

"To retire? Yes, of course, I remember."

"They hit Sal's desk this morning—a month early, fully processed and effective immediately. You know what the odds are against something like that happening?"

"Astronomical," Elsabeth said. She was getting the message, however slowly, and she didn't much like it. "No badge, no gun, you're not a cop anymore. Is that right?"

It hurt to say it but he made himself. "That's right. Now it's strictly personal."

"What is?"

"What made Sal give me the key."

Elsabeth sat back in the seat. She stared straight ahead, hardly breathing. Softly she said, "It isn't over."

Briggs took her hand, holding it firmly in his. "Not until the fat lady sings."

She managed a smile. "Maybe we can give her a nudge."

Briggs glanced behind them out the back window of the bus. He could see people standing around in front of the police station. They were too far away to be seen clearly but he was sure one of them was Leary—the short, skinny one bouncing up and down on the balls of his feet as he flung his arms around wildly.

"I think we just did."

Chapter 12

They left the bus at the Bridgeport train station where they caught a train that took them north to Danbury. Once there they got a taxi to the garage where Briggs kept his extra car. Danbury was very close to Redding and, realizing how near they were, Elsabeth wanted to stop at her house.

"We have to pick up Zared," she insisted. "He can't be left on his own."

"We'll stop in an hour or so. You can call the Cavendishes," Briggs said without slowing down. He liked driving the M.G. Old though it was, the car handled beautifully. For the first time that day he felt better. But there was still Elsabeth to deal with. If the icy silence coming from the passenger seat was any indication, she was fed up.

"When we left this morning," he said mildly, "I put the key under the mat and turned the alarm off. They can get in without any trouble."

"You knew we weren't going back?"

"I had a fair idea," he admitted.

"Why didn't you tell me?"

"Because I hoped I was wrong and there wasn't any point in worrying you."

"I see." More silence, even icier this time. He was beginning to regret not having brought a sweater... earmuffs... a parka.

"Is that all you're going to say?"

"Yes."

"If you're upset, you shouldn't keep it to yourself. That's not good for you."

She turned and looked at him with such regal disdain that he couldn't help but feel a spurt of admiration. No doubt about it, life with her would never be dull.

He almost said as much but the moment didn't seem quite right. She was spitting mad, they were being hunted by a slimy Assistant D.A. and unscrupulous Feds, and there was still the matter of Dickinson's murder to be dealt with.

Besides, the M.G. was too small for the all-out, no-holds-barred knockdown she was clearly itching for. It would have to wait.

They drove for an hour before Briggs thought it safe enough to pull into a rest stop. Elsabeth called Mrs. Cavendish and was assured she would be happy to look after Zared.

"Why, I just love cats," she said, "and you've always been so nice to the twins, it's the least I can do."

Elsabeth felt a twinge of guilt but suppressed it firmly. Briggs had assured her the Cavendishes would be in no danger—although he did think their phone might have been tapped. That was so routine in his book as to barely raise an eyebrow. So far as he was concerned, the real action had moved elsewhere. Still, she hung up quickly before she could give herself much time to wonder what Zared would make of the situation, not to speak of the unsuspecting Mrs. Cavendish. Maybe it was better she didn't know.

After she broke the connection, she waited a moment and punched the numbers for the Red Rooster. Hermione answered on the third ring.

"Gosh, honey, we've all been so worried about you. Are you all right?"

"I'm fine, thanks. Is Mike there?"

"Hold on a sec, I'll go see."

The "sec" dragged out to several minutes before Hermione finally returned. She was breathing hard, as if she'd run all over the restaurant searching for him. "I thought for sure he was here," she said, "but I guess he isn't. But, what the skittles, as long as you're okay. That's what counts."

"Will you tell him for me that I won't be able to come in to work for a while?" She didn't feel right leaving Mike in the lurch but she also didn't imagine he'd be too surprised, especially not after the business with Alphonse. He'd figured she was scared and he'd be right.

On an impulse she asked, "Has anybody heard from Alphonse?"

"Not yet. He said he'd be in touch when he got to San Juan. Say, how did you know about his mom being so sick?"

Elsabeth was silent for a long moment. Her stomach tightened painfully. Slowly she said, "Oh, I just heard. I hope she'll be better soon."

"Yeah, so do I. Alphonse sure was upset when he got the news. Mike was super about it. He bought him a plane ticket and even took him to the airport."

"Super." Her head was reeling. The burly owner of the Red Rooster had always seemed a decent, honorable man. It was all but impossible to imagine him conniving with criminals. All but.

"Everything all right?" Briggs asked when she got back in the car.

"I'm not sure." Briefly she told him what she'd learned about Alphonse.

Briggs cursed under his breath. He was getting a very bad feeling. The same kind he always got walking into a dark alley when he didn't know what he'd encounter there but was certain it wouldn't be good.

"Sal told you about Alphonse disappearing, didn't he?" Elsabeth asked.

Briggs nodded grimly.

"Do you think he believed it?"

"Are you asking me if he can be trusted?"

"Yes, I guess I am. That is what it comes down to, isn't it?"

"I've known Sal for ten years. He's as straight as they come." Even as he said the words he was wondering how true they actually were. He'd have bet money—if he did that kind of thing—on Sal being strictly up-front. He had risked his life going into those same dark alleys he'd been thinking about with only Sal to back him. He'd do it again, but Elsabeth's life . . . that was a whole different story.

"I would have said the same thing about Mike even though I haven't known him anywhere near that long."

"Sal could have just been repeating what he was told by Leary and Stevens. I got the impression they cut him out of the loop pretty thoroughly."

Elsabeth frowned. "What does that mean?"

"That once the Feds came in, the local police weren't really kept informed of what was going on or why. Sal called to warn us because he didn't like what he suspected was going on, namely you being used as bait to flush out Dickinson's killers. Not the little fish but whoever's really behind it all."

"Do you have any ideas on that score?" Elsabeth asked.

Briggs shook his head. "No, but I'm working on it. In the meantime, I wouldn't rule out the possibility that Mike was tricked. Leary and Stevens needed to cover themselves on how Chumpster and the others found out about you. They wouldn't want that laid directly at their door so they arranged for Alphonse to disappear. All they would have had to do was say the authorities needed his cooperation and my guess is Mike would go along. He's the typical good citizen type who isn't inclined to ask too many questions. And Alphonse certainly wasn't in any position to ask questions. How many freebie trips home does a dish-washer get?"

He spoke as confidently as he could, hoping she wouldn't sense the unease he felt. Sal knew where they were headed. If Briggs was wrong and he had been turned, they were walking straight into a trap.

"Look," Briggs said, "we're not going to figure any of this out now. Why don't you get a little rest?"

The idea was tempting. She was worn out in mind and body. Besides, he was right. The answers were going to have to wait. With a little sigh, she settled more comfortably in her seat and shut her eyes.

He shot her a sidelong glance, thinking how beautiful she looked and remembering how that beauty had been heightened even further by passion. He'd spent most of his adult life protecting other people—when all was said and done that's what being a cop meant. He'd always cared about what he was doing but never with such all-consuming intensity. Leary and Stevens had made a bad mistake setting up Elsabeth. They hadn't counted on how far Briggs would go to protect her.

But they were about to find out.

Elsabeth woke hours later. It was still daylight. The car was bumping down a dirt road framed on either side by flat farmland. There was no sign of the highway.

"Where are we?" she asked.

"Toucarow, New Hampshire," Briggs said.

"New Hampshire? What happened to Maine?"

"I changed my mind."

She sat up straighter as the last remnants of sleep vanished, leaving her mind painfully clear. "You decided you weren't sure about Sal after all."

"I decided it wasn't worth the risk. We need to keep a very low profile until I can figure out what to do next."

"By the looks of it, Toucarow, New Hampshire, fits the bill. How did you know about this place, anyway?"

"I extradited a guy from here once."

"Extradited?"

"Brought him back to stand trial in Connecticut. I came up here to get him."

"What was he on trial for?"

"He chopped up his bookie. Left him in pieces all over Bridgeport. We're still finding parts—"

He saw her cringe and cursed himself mentally for being an insensitive clod. "Sorry. Anyway, Toucarow's a great little town."

"This from a man who has nothing good to say about the boonies?"

"The boonies are boring, or at least I used to think they were. Toucarow's got a lot of history. It was founded about a hundred years ago by a religious cult that believed in polyandry."

"Women having more than one husband?"

"Up on that, are you?"

"Georgette was up on *everything* like that. So what happened to the cult?"

"I think they all died from exhaustion."

"Cute. Where's there to stay around here?"

"Fulfillment Cabins and Resort."

"You're making that up," Elsabeth said accusingly.

"I don't have a good enough imagination. Apparently the cult was founded on the idea that what was wrong with the world was people not being, uh, fulfilled. They figured that if everyone was—you know—"

"Getting enough?"

"You could put it that way. They figured nobody would have any time to fight wars or otherwise cause trouble."

"Actually, it's not such a bad idea."

"About all that's left of it are the cabins."

"I can't wait," Elsabeth muttered. "I positively cannot wait."

Briggs grinned. "Sorry, honey, you're just gonna have to."

Elsabeth glared at him, but then she knew he'd be disappointed if she didn't. She really had to admire the man, going that far out on the edge with a woman who had her own guillotine. Gutsy, that's what he was. Or nutsy. She was getting those two confused.

He was right about one thing, though, it didn't look as if Toucarow would be boring.

Fulfillment Cabins was half a mile down the road. A hand-painted sign that read Office hung above the door of a whitewashed cottage. In front of the cottage and all around it, roses bloomed in profusion. They grew along the white picket fence, up the arching trellises and over the low stone walls. Their potent, almost dizzying perfume filled the air. Off to the side in an open meadow, wildflowers flourished. Elsabeth glimpsed cowslip, snakeroot, Indian blanket, asters and more before she gave up, shaking her head in amazement. "Good Lord," she murmured.

"Wait," Briggs said. "It gets better." He opened the door and stood aside to let her enter. A cozy front room held a potbellied stove with rocking chairs clustered around it. Shelves built into the walls were filled with skeins of brilliantly colored wool. A half-finished sweater lay on one of the rockers. Nearby was a wooden counter polished to a high sheen by years of use. Behind the counter, a rack of hooks held a dozen or so keys.

"There's no one here," Elsabeth said, looking around.

"Is that a fact?" A tuft of white hair appeared above the counter, followed by a cherubic face set off by bright brown eyes nestled behind wire-rimmed glasses. The eyes—and the glasses—belonged to a small, round person dressed in paisley and lace, which stood out against an immense apron wrapped around her ample middle. She smelled of cinnamon and lemon oil, and she smiled when she saw Briggs.

"Why, Detective Caldwell, this is a nice surprise. Have you come to arrest someone again?"

"Not this time, Miss Olivia. My friend and I are on a little vacation and I convinced her Toucarow was worth a visit."

"Oh my, I should say it is." The little old lady looked Elsabeth up and down approvingly. "Yes, I should say so. Just the place for you. And so much nicer than running after nasty murderers. Didn't we tell you that you should stop all that and write that book you had in mind?"

"You did," Briggs agreed, "and you were certainly right. By the way, how is Miss Lavinia?"

"Dreadful as ever, but never you mind. Now let me see, where shall we put you?"

She turned back to the key rack while Elsabeth shot a look at Briggs. He returned it squarely, leaving no doubt as to where he stood. He was a cop—even if he was recently retired—doing his job, which was keeping her alive. He couldn't do that if they were in separate rooms. If she wanted to make a fuss about it, that was okay by him but it wouldn't change a thing.

All that in a single look. Heaven help her, she was really getting to know the man.

Heaven help him, too, if only he'd known it. Making a fuss was the furthest thing from her mind.

"Ah, here we are," Miss Olivia said. "Number Seven, always my favorite. I'm sure you'll be very comfortable." She handed the key to him with a flourish.

Briggs thanked her gravely. "By the way, we left in a kind of a hurry. Any chance Sherman's still open?"

Miss Olivia's eyes twinkled. "Ah, youth, so impetuous. I remember how it was when I was a girl, so exciting when dear Robert and Samuel and Jacob were alive. But then, life does go on. I'll give Sherman a call and tell him you're coming over."

Briggs thanked her again before taking Elsabeth's arm and ushering her back outside to the car. "All right," she said, "I'll bite. Who's Sherman and why are we going to see him? And while we're at it, who are *dear* Robert, Samuel and Jacob?"

"Remember what I told you about this place?" Briggs asked as he slid behind the wheel.

Elsabeth's eyes widened. "You mean—?"

"Miss Olivia and her sister, Lavinia, are all that's left of the group that first founded Toucarow. Robert, Samuel and Jacob were Olivia's husbands. Lavinia had three of her own but I can't remember their names."

"That sweet old lady," Elsabeth murmured.

"Probably knows more about certain things than you or I ever will. Sherman, by the way, is her great-nephew. He runs a sort of all-purpose store. I figured we could use a few things."

"Since we left in kind of a hurry," Elsabeth mimicked. "You purposely misled her into thinking that this was some great flight of passion instead of a simple desire to stay alive."

"Don't kid yourself," Briggs said. "Olivia's sharp as a tack. Nobody puts anything over on her or Lavinia."

"You can believe that if you want to, but—"

"You know that book she mentioned encouraging me to write?"

"What about it?"

"I never told her or her sister that I had any interest in writing when I was here before. They just dropped that on me out of the clear blue sky." He grinned at her surprise. "Aren't you the person who believes in magic?"

"I guess…" She pondered that as they drove the short distance to Sherman's Grocery and Emporium, a ramshackle wooden building occupying a wide spot along the road. Sherman came out to greet them personally. He was an owlish man of middle years with eyes as brown as Olivia's and a gentle smile.

"Come on in," he said as they walked up the steps to the entrance framed by barrels of apples slumbering in the fading sun.

"Nice to see you again, Mr. Caldwell," Sherman said. He waved a hand vaguely in the direction of the shelves. "Help yourself to whatever you need. There's a cigar box with change on the counter."

"Thanks," Briggs said. "What are you reading these days, Sherman?"

The mild face lit up, transforming the Milquetoast man with the vitality of enthusiasm. "Sophocles. I'm working my way through all the plays again. It's well worth the effort. You might enjoy it sometime yourself."

"I'm sure I would," Briggs said lightly. "Unfortunately I'd have to read them in translation."

Sherman looked bemused for a moment before he nodded. "Oh, of course, I forget. Well, if you'll excuse me..."

"What does he forget?" Elsabeth asked when they were alone.

"That this isn't the nineteenth century when any man with pretensions to being educated can read Greek. Sherman used to teach at Yale but he found the environment heavy going so he came back here instead. He still writes for scholarly journals and he runs this store, more or less. But most of his time he spends reading."

"Not a bad life, I guess."

"Not for him," Briggs agreed. "Come on, let's get what we need."

They added up their purchases carefully and deposited the money in the cigar box. On their way out they called a goodbye to Sherman who may or may not have heard them.

"What next?" Elsabeth asked.

"Dinner," Briggs said.

On cue, her stomach growled. She laughed. "I like a man who has his priorities straight. First, stay alive. Second, get comfortable. Third, eat."

"We'll discuss fourth later," Briggs said.

A frisson of anticipation darted through her. She flushed slightly but refrained from comment.

Chapter 13

They ate at a diner half a mile down the road from Sherman's. The place served truckers coming through on the interstate and a handful of locals. The menu was strictly meat and potatoes, but the food was fresh and well prepared.

Elsabeth was surprised by how hungry she was until she remembered that she hadn't eaten since the previous day. Digging into a slice of peach pie, she stole a glance at Briggs. Unlike her, he had only toyed with his food. There were dark shadows under his eyes and he looked bone tired.

Her conscience troubled her as she realized that he had borne the brunt of responsibility over the last few days. He'd had to make some very tough decisions while confronting an enemy who was still unknown. And he'd done it all with great courage and consider-

ation for her, even if he did tend to be just a bit pre-
sumptuous.

"Briggs," she said softly, waking him from his rev-
erie, "let's go back to the cabin."

She left the pie unfinished and quickly scooped up
the check. That he let her do so drove home to her just
how tired and distracted he really was.

"I'll drive if you like," she offered when they were
back in the parking lot.

"No, I'm fine, really. I just want to get this thing
figured out."

They drove back to Fulfillment in silence. Briggs
was once again grateful that Elsabeth wasn't a woman
who needed to be reassured constantly or entertained.
A woman he could be quiet with, who allowed him the
privacy of his own thoughts, was a new experience. He
found himself relishing it.

Still, there was no getting around the fact that he
needed rest. It would disappoint Olivia and Lavinia
something awful if they knew that, but there wasn't
anything to be done about it. Ruefully he acknowledged to himself that he wasn't a kid anymore.

It was dark by the time they got back to the cabins.
A cooling breeze blew off the mountains to the north.
The air was scented with sleeping roses and the wild-
flowers of the meadow.

Briggs opened the door to the cabin and stepped
inside to let Elsabeth in. She stood stock-still, unable
to hide her surprise. Ahead lay a small but beautifully
proportioned room. The walls were of hand-hewn
planks, the floor of fieldstone, and the simple, pine
furniture looked like the kind country antique dealers
would give their right arm for. A colorful, star-

patterned quilt covered the large bed. Braided rugs dotted the floor. Bunches of dried flowers and herbs hung from the rafters, filling the room with their fragrance. At the far end of the cabin an overstuffed couch faced a potbellied stove. An iron kettle next to it held kindling.

"This is wonderful," Elsabeth said softly. "How is it more people don't know about this place?"

"I guess because Olivia and Lavinia are happy with things just the way they are," Briggs said. "People happen by, find out what's here, and end up coming back. Those two old ladies believe a lot in fate—they think if you're meant to be here, you will be."

"I can't wait to meet Lavinia," Elsabeth said with a grin. Someone, Olivia, she supposed, had placed an urn with fresh flowers on a table near the door. The thoughtful gesture warmed her.

She used the bathroom first, emerging enveloped in the old-fashioned white cotton nightgown she'd bought at Sherman's. Briggs grinned when he saw her. Her hair was freshly brushed and gleaming, tumbling down her shoulders. Her face was scrubbed free of makeup, the skin glowing. She looked at once unbearably beautiful and heart-stoppingly innocent.

Maybe it was just as well he was exhausted, Briggs thought. He had a hell of a time controlling himself where she was concerned.

When he came out of the bathroom a short while later, the lights were off in the cabin. He could see the soft rise in the bed that was Elsabeth. The other side was neatly turned down and waiting for him.

Either she was the most tactful woman this side of heaven or she was as worn out as he was. Whichever

was the case, he wasn't about to quibble. He slipped
into bed beside her, laid his head on the pillow and was
instantly asleep.

Briggs woke to the touch of warm, moist lips trailing down his bare chest. He lay in the half state between dreams and consciousness, and let the heat curl
through him. Feathery silk brushed over him, along
his rib cage and the flat span of his abdomen. He lifted
his hands slowly, feeling no need for haste, and wove
them through Elsabeth's hair. She murmured softly
and continued her exploration.

Her heart was beating very fast, partly from her
own arousal but also from her daring. She had never
been so bold in her life but what drew her to this man
was simply too powerful to resist. It banished every
other consideration and brought out a part of herself
that both shocked and delighted her.

If the low groans of pleasure coming from Briggs
were anything to go by, he didn't mind too much. Her
mouth curved in a smile as old as woman. She drew
back and lifted the long cotton gown over her head,
dispensing with it in a single movement.

In the gray half-light of predawn, her body was al-
abaster shadowed by fire. The red-gold tumble of hair
over her shoulders was echoed in the soft triangle between her thighs. Her breasts were high and full, the
nipples hardened. She trembled slightly, rocked by
wave after wave of desire.

Her hands and her mouth returned to him. Delicately, following instincts she hadn't known she possessed, she dropped hot, tiny kisses along the length of
his throat to the broad sweep of his shoulders. She felt

the power of his heated muscles beneath her and sensed how sternly he was holding himself in check. The license he gave her prompted her to go even further.

Her fingers were cool and strong against the cord of his pajama bottoms. They brushed over his swollen manhood as she slipped the garment away. Sitting back on her knees, she studied him appreciatively. "You are a beautiful man."

"Want to guess what else I am?" Briggs asked through gritted teeth.

Elsabeth gave him a playful smile. "Cold?"

"Wrong."

"Still sleepy?"

"Wrong."

"Gee, I can't imagine..."

He moved so quickly that she barely had time to draw a breath. One moment she was above him, gently teasing, and the next she was flat on her back, pressed into the mattress with an intensely aroused male poised above her.

"Oh, that," she murmured as he moved against her, making her vividly aware of his desire.

"Yeah," Briggs growled deep in his throat. "That."

"What a coincidence," Elsabeth said. Her legs parted slightly, inviting him into the warm, wet heat of her.

Briggs smiled against her skin but he wasn't ready to end their play yet. Instead he drew the pleasure out, tormenting them both exquisitely. His teeth raked the delicate flesh of her nipples, eliciting small cries of ecstasy. He suckled her urgently, laving the swell of her breasts with his tongue. His hand slipped between her legs, stroking the small, hard bud concealed in the fiery nest.

Elsabeth cried out sharply, twisting beneath him. "Enough," she breathed, reaching for him.

Briggs caught her wrists, holding her captive. He moved down the length of her body, following his hand until his mouth found her most sensitive point. Tiny whimpers of pleasure broke from her. He drew it out, waiting...waiting...until neither of them could bear anything more. Only then did he spread her legs wide and surge within her.

Long, slow strokes of his manhood moving deep inside her drove Elsabeth over the edge of consciousness and beyond. She cried out his name, her head thrashing on the pillows, distantly aware of his voice joining hers. His life spilled into her, a homage to her womanhood, before they both collapsed, spent and exhausted.

Briggs began to shift his weight off Elsabeth but she stopped him. "Stay," she whispered, "I like the way you feel."

He subsided back into her arms, his eyes closed and his spirit at peace. Distantly, in the back of his mind, this tough, no-nonsense man knew he had never felt so cherished.

Elsabeth's hand stroked his back softly. Her breath was warm against him. He raised himself on his elbows and looked down into her crystalline eyes.

"I love you," he said.

Her eyes pooled, turning luminous. There was a catch in her throat as she said, "That's the nicest thing anyone's ever said to me. By the way, I love you, too."

Which set them both to laughing in the way people will when they are totally, overwhelmingly happy.

They stayed two days in Toucarow. Most of that time was spent in the cabin, reconfirming their feelings for each other in ways both big and small. They made love often but they also sat in front of the pot-bellied stove, welcome on the cool nights, playing checkers, reading or talking. They went for walks in the pine forests beyond the fields and bathed together in the big, claw-footed tub that took up most of the bathroom.

The diner kept them fed, the sisters provided privacy, and the peace and simplicity of the place wound itself around them like a soft, welcoming blanket. The world, with all of its tribulations, seemed very far away.

In fact, it was as close as the other end of a phone call. The second day they were there, Elsabeth called the Cavendishes to check on Zared.

"Oh, he's just fine," Mrs. Cavendish assured her. "The twins love having him here and, of course, we do, too."

"Having him there?" Elsabeth asked.

"I hope you don't mind but we thought it best to bring him over. The man at your house said it would be all right."

"What man?"

"He, uh, he said he was your cousin. He said you knew he was staying there. That's true, isn't it?"

Swiftly, to allay the other woman's obvious alarm, Elsabeth said, "Sure, of course, I just forgot for a sec. Well, thanks again."

"When are you coming back?" Mrs. Cavendish asked quickly as she sensed Elsabeth was about to hang up.

"Soon. If Zared gets to be too much for you, you can leave him at the vet's. They actually get along pretty well."

"Oh, no, that won't be necessary..."

Briggs was making gestures to end the conversation. Hastily Elsabeth said, "Whatever you think best. Thanks again. Bye."

She hung up before Mrs. Cavendish could ask anything more and exhaled sharply.

"There's a man at my house. He told her he's my cousin."

"I'm sorry," Briggs said, knowing how much she would hate having her privacy invaded.

Abruptly she smiled, surprising him. "I hope he stays away from the guillotine, among other things."

Briggs's eyebrows rose. "Other things?"

She looked at him through her lashes. Her voice dropped, becoming low and sultry. "Things I cannot speak of. Things best left unsaid. Things that—"

"Go bump in the night?" Briggs asked, laughing.

"Oh, no, if one could hear them, one might have a chance of escape, however slim. But when the domain of the *magicienne* is intruded upon, one cannot be held responsible for what happens to one, can one?"

"How many ones is that?"

"Enough to know better. Whoever the guy is, he better keep his mitts off my stuff or he'll rue the day he got turned into a rabbit."

"Can you really do that?"

"Want me to try?"

"Not this minute." He put an arm around her, drawing her close. His head bent, his breath touching her cheek lightly. She could feel the warmth of his mouth so near...

"Let's go back to the cabin," he said.

Briggs left her sleeping. He slipped out the door and got into the car, driving the short distance to the diner. In the pay phone next to it, he punched in his credit card number followed by the number he wanted. He was taking a chance but there wasn't much choice. They were running out of alternatives.

Sal answered on the first ring as though he had been waiting by the phone.

"You lit a fire here, pal. Leary and Stevens are going nuts."

"Is it true they picked up the Stick?" Briggs asked.

"Yeah, I saw him in Holding. Listen, I gotta call you back, I don't like this phone. I tried, you know, the place we talked about and there was no answer. You change your plans?"

Briggs hesitated. He'd meant to keep the conversation short, as he'd instructed Elsabeth to do. If Sal was on the up-and-up, Leary and Stevens might easily have tapped his line. Of course, if he wasn't, letting him know where they were would be the worst thing to do.

"Come on," Sal said, "what's the problem?" He was silent for a moment as he figured it out for himself. "You really think I could be in with those creeps?" He sounded more hurt than angry, which was hard to imagine since Sal had the skin of your average rhinoceros. Still, everyone had feelings.

"I don't know, Sal," Briggs replied. "I'm just trying to be careful."

"Who gave you the gun? You think I did that so you'd get hurt? Geez, what am I doing mentioning that on this line? You got me going crazy."

"I'm sorry, Sal. Look, what do you and me need to talk about, anyway? We're just going to stay low and wait this out, so there's really nothing more for you to—"

"You think so? You don't know nothing. Things are going down here so fast you blink and you miss something. We *gotta* talk. You hear that? *Gotta.*"

"I hear," Briggs said slowly. He had to make a decision and make it fast. Trust Sal or not? He took a deep breath and said, "You remember Charlie Carver?"

"Charlie who?"

"Carver. The Carver. You remember him?"

"Wait a minute...the guy...it was a stinking hot summer...you and me hanging out at McHenry's?"

"That's it." Briggs and Sal had been having a drink together at a joint called McHenry's when they got word of the bookie's murder. They'd been coming off an overtime shift and the last thing they'd needed was more action. They'd cursed "Numbers" roundly until they'd seen what had happened to him. After that, all they'd cared about was finding his killer.

Charlie Carver was the murderer's street name, not the way he was indexed in the arrest records. The department had always meant to cross-reference the files but there had never been enough money to do it. Which meant that anyone listening in would have to go through Briggs's entire service record before even having a chance of figuring out what they were talking about.

"Remember that little place I told you about?"

"The broads who...you know?" Sal had been particularly taken with the notion of Toucarow. He'd talked about going up to take a look for himself but he'd never gotten around to it. Now he laughed under his breath. "Geez, you got a great sense of humor."

"It just fit the ticket, that's all," Briggs claimed, inwardly denying that he'd known Elsabeth would find Toucarow particularly interesting, maybe even enough to divert her thoughts from the danger they faced.

He'd called Sal several times while chasing Carver and had always used the diner's phone because it offered the most anonymity. There'd be a record of the number in Carver's arrest record. Sal would know where to find it.

"Wait there," Sal said. "I need five minutes."

Briggs waited. He thought about calling the cabins and getting a message to Elsabeth that they had to pull out but decided against it. Either he trusted Sal or he didn't. He'd always managed to maintain some degree of emotional distance between himself and the world but that wasn't working anymore. He was in love with Elsabeth, he was vulnerable, and he had to make the best of it that he could.

So he waited, pacing up and down beside the phone booth. For the first time in years, he wished he still smoked.

The phone rang. Briggs yanked it off the hook.

"Yeah," he said.

"Ever hear of a place called Waterside Warehousing?" Sal asked.

"Yeah, sure. It's down by the ferry. We fished Dommy Lucaso out of the water near there a couple of years back, or what was left of him."

"That's the place. Seems Mick the Stick, Dapper Dan and the Chumpster are all on the Waterside payroll. They got social security numbers, withholding, insurance, the works. I ran it through the computer and it came up clear."

"And?"

"Waterside Warehousing is owned by something called National Properties, Inc."

"Never heard of it," Briggs said.

"It's a wholly owned subsidiary of Transcom International."

"Doesn't ring a bell."

"Which is a Cayman Island-based holding company for Hodding Industries. Sound familiar?"

Briggs frowned. He did have a faint recollection somewhere way in the back of his mind. Something that had left a bad taste...something outside his usual experience, but...

"Wait a minute, is that the guy the Feds thought was running arms to the Libyans but they couldn't get anything on him?"

"Give the man a cigar," Sal said. "Ol' Fairley Wilson Hodding the Third, Hod, to his pals of whom he undoubtedly has many. 'Course, they're not the kind of folks most of us would want to associate with, but ol' Hod isn't too particular. Long as you've got the bucks, he's got the bang."

"Yeah," Briggs said softly, "I got him now. He was involved in that mess in the Mulgasy Republic where damn near the whole capital city got wiped out. He supplied the missiles, didn't he? And then there was South Africa, Sri Lanka, El Salvador, Lebanon. The Feds had a list a mile long but they couldn't make anything stick."

"Mr. Hodding has the benefit of very expensive lawyers who know how to earn their keep. But he's also apparently got a temper. Seems he and the late Mr. Dickinson had a falling out and ol' Hod decided he didn't want the numbers man hanging around. Least that's what Mickey-boy says."

So much for the idea that Dickinson had caught Mickey and the others skimming. Stevens had tried hard to sell that one, but Briggs hadn't believed him. Now he was glad.

"You talked to Mick?"

"In Holding, but privatelike."

Briggs didn't even want to ask what strings Sal had pulled to manage that. Or what kind of persuasion he'd used. "What did they argue about?" he asked.

"Don't know. Neither one of them took Mickey-boy into his confidence. He just got the job to waste Dickinson. He says he brought in Dan and the Chumpster to help, but my guess is he's just blowing himself up. Odds are Dapper ran the operation and Mick was just the hired help."

"So where does that leave us on an indictment?"

"It leaves us with zippo. On the one hand, Mick's a repeat offender looking at very hard time. He's got enough incentive to sell us his grandmother, presuming he ever had one. *But* a first-year law student would eat him up alive, let alone the heavy guns Hodding can call up." More softly Sal said, "I'm sorry, pal, but just hang in there. With a little luck—"

"You're not talking luck, Sal. You're talking flat-out miracle. Hodding's stayed loose for years. What makes you think we can take him now?"

There was silence for a moment before Sal said, "'Cause we gotta, buddy. We just gotta. A creep like that running around, forget keeping the streets safe. The whole damn planet's up for grabs. You want your kids living with that?"

"I don't have any kids," Briggs said automatically. His brain was on overdrive, trying to figure out an angle. He wasn't having much luck.

"Not now you don't but what about a few years from now? You ever think of that? You want somebody like Hod running around then?"

"Of course I don't," Briggs said. "I know the guy is scum. I know he has to be taken out. The question is how to do it. Clowns like Stevens and Leary aren't my top choices for the job."

"Mine neither," Sal muttered. "Look, it's okay. You sit tight. I'll work it out."

"What are you talking about, *you'll* work it out?"

"You remember my cousin Lucia whose kid got killed on that plane that had a bomb on it?"

"Yeah," Briggs said softly. "I remember." The Christmas Eve explosion of a major commercial aircraft over the North Atlantic had stunned the world. Everyone knew terrorists were behind it, but no one had ever paid for the deaths of more than two hundred Americans, many of them college students returning home from studying abroad.

"You think I can look her in the face while a guy like Hod, a guy who sells to those creeps, is still running around loose?"

"Listen, Sal," Briggs said quickly, "what did you always tell me? Don't let it get personal. It gets personal, you get dead. Isn't that right?"

There was a long silence before Sal said, "Sometimes you change your mind about what really matters, pal. Something hits you in the face and you know what you gotta do. It's the kids, is what it is. They're what count."

"Sal, listen to me, there's no way you can handle something like this on your own. You've got to be reasonable. You've got to—"

Briggs broke off. He was talking to empty space. Sal had hung up.

Chapter 14

"**H**e did what?" Elsabeth asked disbelievingly. She was standing in the office in front of the counter. Olivia had taken one look at her, sighed piteously, and ducked out of sight. Her sister, Lavinia, was made of sterner stuff.

"He went back to Connecticut," the tall, reed-thin woman in the no-nonsense gray dress said. She was about the same age as Olivia, anywhere between sixty and a hundred, and had the same stock of white hair above her bright brown eyes. Other than that, they could not have been more dissimilar. Olivia was tea and cinnamon buns in a cozy kitchen; Lavinia was chalk and castor oil in a frontier schoolhouse.

"He couldn't have," Elsabeth said. "There's no way he would have gone off and left me here."

Lavinia shrugged. "He said you'd be in good hands and he'd be in touch soon. He also said you wouldn't be happy about this and to bear with you as best we could."

"*Sister,*" Olivia protested, popping up from behind the counter, "that isn't at all polite. Detective Caldwell was called back on business. He'll return as soon as he can and I'm sure that won't be long. In the meantime, we'll take the very best care of you." She looked at her sister pointedly. "We promised."

"Looks perfectly capable of taking care of herself, if you ask me," Lavinia said. "A lot of fuss over nothing."

"Oh, what do you know about it?" Olivia demanded. In a stage whisper Elsabeth could not possibly miss, she added, "I think it's terribly romantic. Besides, he's such a nice young man."

"You think any young man is nice," Lavinia said caustically. "You always did."

"You weren't exactly a shrinking violet yourself," Olivia shot back. "Why, I remember when you first met dear Francis, the play you made for him, the poor man barely knew what hit him."

Lavinia drew herself upright and looked down her formidable nose. "The poor man, as you called him, died in his bed at the age of eighty-two with—I might add—a smile on his face. Which is more than I can say for your Jacob."

Olivia's face flushed. "Oh, how bad of you to throw that up to me! As though I were to blame for his falling off the wagon the way he did."

"He had a drinking problem?" Elsabeth asked, trying to follow the conversation.

"He liked his dandelion wine, all right," Lavinia said. "But no, he wasn't really a drinking man. He fell off a wagon, a mule wagon he had no business being on in the first place. Not that you could tell him a thing. Headstrong, he was.''

"That was part of his charm," Olivia sniffed. "You wouldn't understand. Always wanting to be the bossy one. Well, let me tell you, there's going to come a day when I'm not going to stand for that anymore. If you think—''

Elsabeth tiptoed out, leaving them still arguing. She had her own thinking to do. Briggs had taken the car, leaving her neatly stranded. But she was going to change that if she had to sprout wings and fly. Somewhere in Martha Byrnes's old book there were probably instructions for how to do that. Heaven knew, there were plenty of other peculiar things.

The book had been in her pocket when she accompanied Briggs to the police station to give their reports. She'd brought it along thinking that if they got stuck, she'd have something to read. As it was, the days in Toucarow had given her the chance to study it in depth when she wasn't otherwise engaged. There was still much she didn't understand and more she didn't believe, but she was still itching to try her hand at a few of the less outrageous "recipes."

For the more outrageous ones, she'd wait until she had Briggs back to test them on. He deserved it.

She walked the half mile to Sherman's, finding the place deserted as usual. Sherman was in the back, stretched out in a hammock hung between two ancient maple trees. At least his body was there. His mind was somewhere back in ancient Greece.

"Hi, there," Elsabeth said, urging it back.

No response. The hammock swayed, the birds sang, and Sherman kept reading.

Elsabeth sighed. She drew a bird from her hand and placed it on his nose.

"Oh, hello," he said, sitting up. The bird vanished with a flick of her wrist.

"Nice, that," Sherman murmured. "I can't imagine how you do it."

"Unfortunately there are limits. For instance, I'd love to be able to conjure a taxi right about now but I can't. Is one available anywhere around here?"

"A taxi?" He repeated the word as though it was completely foreign to him. "Oh, no, I don't think so. People around here don't have much use for that sort of thing."

"How about a car I could rent?" Elsabeth went on. "I'd pay very well."

"But doesn't Detective Caldwell have a car—"

"He does. I'd like my own. Any ideas?"

"Well, let's see." He thought for a while before he shook his head. "I'm afraid not. I'm not awfully good at this kind of thing. But if you want to go somewhere, why don't you just take the bus?"

"Bus?" Elsabeth echoed. It hadn't occurred to her that such a thing existed.

Sherman nodded. "Comes through every afternoon. Stops at the diner. In fact—" he glanced at his watch "—I could run you down there right now, if you like. You still have time to make it."

Elsabeth would have hugged him except she knew how embarrassed he'd be. Instead she contented herself by entrusting him with a message for Olivia and Lavinia, to wit that she would be back as soon as possible to pay the bill and collect her things but if there was any problem with that, they should just go ahead and charge everything to her. She gave Sherman her credit card number even though he insisted it wasn't necessary.

"There's no rush," he said. "Once people find this place, they tend to come back. It may take a while but sooner or later they all show up again."

What he said made Elsabeth wonder when she, too, would be coming back to Toucarow. With Briggs, she hoped, since she couldn't imagine being there without him. Of course, she'd reached the point where she couldn't imagine being without him period. Not that he wasn't the most infuriating man she'd ever met. He was going to hear about that the moment she found him.

All she had to do now was figure out where he'd gone. Bridgeport was a fair guess but that was a big place. She couldn't very well go waltzing into the police station or ask Leary for help. There had to be another way.

She decided to start at his apartment. The bus got her in early the next morning after a distinctly uncomfortable night. She treated herself to a cup of coffee at the luncheonette in the station, then went outside to get a cab, blessing her own foresight at always carrying ample amounts of cash. Georgette had drummed that into her. "A girl should always have a spare hundred or two for emergencies, dear." Much later Elsabeth had found out that most mothers told their daughters to carry a dime so they could make a call in case of trouble. Trust Georgette to go them a whole lot better.

Trust her to be right, too.

She paid the cabbie off and walked up the path to the condominium complex. It was a bright, clear day. Seagulls whirled in the sky above, their raucous cries colliding with the soft, fleecy clouds that hovered near the sun but did not hide it. A sense of well-being flowed through Elsabeth. She would find Briggs soon, they would sort everything out, they would—what? Her imagination did not extend quite that far. She wouldn't let it. Enough for the moment to be content with the day and with the man who had awakened her to a life more beautiful and meaningful than any she had ever known.

She was smiling, her eyes alight with thoughts of him, when a shadow stepped away from the building. Elsabeth had a moment to know something had gone terribly wrong before pain fractured her consciousness. A great, yawning maw opened beneath her. She screamed once and fell into it.

Briggs cursed under his breath. He was crouched around the corner from Waterside Warehousing, a block-long structure hugging the river in one of the seedier parts of Bridgeport. Sections of the city had undergone urban renewal, some of them more successfully than others. But this particular area still awaited the wrecking ball. While it did, it attracted the blind eye of officials other than the police who kept a wary eye on goings-on, usually after dark.

In late afternoon the surrounding area was virtually deserted. A few boats drifted by on the river and far off in the distance the sound of a fire engine siren could be heard. But otherwise nothing moved. It might as well have been high noon on the empty prairie as a business day in a major American city.

Briggs put a hand over his eyes, shading them from the sun, and took another cautious look around. He had been in spots like this before and he knew how deceptive they could be. There were plenty of streets like this one, plenty of places where strangers didn't go and questions weren't asked. Places where a solitary cop had to be crazy to hang around for very long.

Or so worried about a friend that he forgot all the basic rules of self-preservation.

He had been watching the warehouse for half an hour and in that time only a handful of vehicles had passed. But now a black panel truck came halfway down the block and turned into the driveway. A man got out of the truck and approached the chain-link fence, unlocking the gate. He swung it open, returned to the van and drove through. Meticulously he re-locked the gate before proceeding.

Briggs watched the van disappear around the corner of the loading dock. He had a bad feeling in the pit of his stomach. Ordinarily he'd have waited until dark to make a move. Instead he checked the gun at the small of his back and decided it was all-or-nothing time.

As his old sergeant in Vietnam had said, "Whattaya, wanna live forever?"

He ran in a crouch across the road, ending flat up against the chain-link fence. Although the day was warm, the metal felt cold against his back. He was wearing jeans, a cotton shirt and a denim jacket, the last donned in deference to the gun jammed into his belt. He should have been hot, if anything. But the coldness got through to him and made him realize how much he was about to risk.

He wanted to live, plain and simple. He'd always wanted that but never quite in the same way that he did now. Elsabeth had made the difference. She had injected possibilities into a life hitherto filled only with necessities.

Stay outside, play it safe, and maybe end up with a dead friend and a load on his conscience that would destroy him eventually, Elsabeth's love notwithstanding?

Or go?

He went. Fast and hard, staying low, taking the fence in a leap that carried him halfway up, then over the top in a single heartbeat and dropping the twelve feet to the ground because, what the hell, a bum ankle was better than a shot in the back.

He made it.

Just barely, but he wasn't asking for miracles. Not yet, anyway.

The warehouse was windowless and aside from the loading docks, almost without doors. Briggs found only a single entrance concealed well out of sight of the street. Not unexpectedly, it was locked.

During the course of twenty years on the police force, a man picked up a few tips. The lock was good but not great. It took Briggs all of forty-five seconds to open it. He slid the thin, steel pick back into his pocket and went in.

So far he figured he was good for carrying an illegal weapon and breaking and entering. Not bad for a day's work.

Except for a few partitions, the warehouse stretched unbroken over the full city block. The ceiling was two stories high. Off to one side, a cluster of offices hung above the warehouse floor. Lights were on in one of them.

He went carefully, the desire to live very strong in him now and growing more intense by the moment. To live—him, Sal, Elsabeth—without fear, without the shadow of old business hanging over them. Free.

The thought propelled him up the narrow steps that went not to the office where the lights shone but to the one three down in the line from it, all the way at the end so that it jutted out over the warehouse floor. The office door was unlocked. It creaked slightly as he opened it. He froze for a moment, not moving, before shutting it slowly behind him. The office was dark. It was filled with metal desks and bookshelves that barely looked used. Business might be conducted there occasionally but not on a regular basis. That was in keeping with the warehouse itself, which was empty of all but a few piles of crates set at intervals over the vast floor.

Not exactly a booming business.

Or was it?

There were "goods" that took up very little space, that came and went quickly, and that were immensely profitable. Guns, for example, the smaller missiles suitable for handheld launchers, ammunition of every type, and all the exotic, death-dealing paraphernalia the mad world couldn't seem to do without. Hodding's stock-in-trade.

A small hatch in the office ceiling gave access to its roof. Briggs stood on top of a desk to reach it and squeezed himself through. He lay for a few moments on top of the structure, surveying his surroundings. Insulated cables and metal duct work covered most of the surface. Mounds of dust and debris made the going treacherous. He stood up cautiously and moved forward, careful not to make a sound. When he reached the last office, the one where the lights were on, he paused. Muted voices reached him from below. He couldn't make out the words but the voices were male. They sounded good-humored, even amused.

He didn't like that.

A door slammed. Footsteps sounded on the metal stairs. Not one person, more than that. And heavy. He risked a look, enough to make out a couple of hulking shapes, linebacker types. They crossed the warehouse floor and disappeared in the direction of the loading dock.

Briggs counted to a thousand silently. When he was as sure as he could be that the coast was clear, he lowered himself slowly onto the narrow gantry that ran around the offices. The windows were covered by venetian blinds but they had been left open. He had an unobstructed view inside.

Rage poured through him like molten lava. He fought against it, knowing that now more than ever he needed control. For his sake, and for Elsabeth's and Sal's.

Elsabeth was conscious, he took some reassurance from that. She was tied to a straight-back chair, her mouth taped. Her hair was disheveled and there was a bruise on her right cheek. Her eyes were wide with fear. She was staring at the man in the chair opposite her. Sal was trussed up like her but his mouth was free. Apparently his captors had no fear of him speaking. Briggs could see why. Sal was deeply unconscious, as the result of a brutal beating that had left his face swollen and bloody. His head lolled to one side and his breathing, visible even from across the room, was labored.

Suddenly Elsabeth stiffened. She managed to turn her head so that she could see over her shoulder. For a moment they looked directly at each other. There was no surprise in her eyes. Somehow she had known before she saw him that he was there.

Briggs didn't question that. Later there'd be time for explanations. There had to be. The office door had been left unlocked, further proof if it was needed that Hodding's goons were overly confident.

He went to Elsabeth first. Murmuring an apology, he pulled the tape away from her mouth. She winced but didn't make a sound. Quickly Briggs untied her hands and feet and helped her to stand. For a moment they stood close within each other's arms, savoring the simple fact that they were both alive and together. But other, more urgent matters demanded attention.

"We've got to get him out of here," Elsabeth murmured as Briggs bent over Sal. "They've hurt him terribly."

Briggs nodded grimly. "How long has he been like this?"

"I don't know. I've only been here a few minutes and he was unconscious before then."

"You were in the van, the one that just came in?"

"I guess so. They knocked me out, so I'm not really sure where I was. I came to while they were tying me up." She laid a hand on his arm. "Briggs, it was the two men who were at my house, the Chumpster and Dan Ruglio." A tremor ran through her. "I heard them talking. They were going to kill me. They were only waiting to hear from whoever they were working for."

He drew her close, holding her until the worst of her fear passed. His did not, nor did the rage. A lot would have to happen before that would change.

"I can't understand how they got out of jail so fast," Elsabeth said. She lifted her head and looked at him.

"I can," Briggs replied. There was a light in his eyes that made Elsabeth shy away momentarily. For an instant a flicker of nearly murderous fury brushed over her. It vanished almost before she could be sure of what she had sensed, but the memory lingered. For the first time she realized that Briggs could, when truly pressed, be a very dangerous man. She knew him as a consummately tender and passionate lover, and as a good friend. But there was another side to him, the side of the hunter and the protector, that she preferred not to know too much about.

Together, they untied Sal. The older man groaned faintly but otherwise remained silent and inert. It was impossible to guess the extent of his injuries, only that they were very grave. If his life was to be saved, they had to move quickly.

The question facing Briggs was how? Chumpster and Ruglio could return at any moment. There might be others in different parts of the warehouse. They had to get down the stairs and across an almost empty floor, with few places to hide, without being spotted. That would be tough enough if he had only Elsabeth to worry about, but with a severely injured man to boot, the odds were overwhelmingly against them.

Briggs was debating what to do, looking for an edge however slight, when Elsabeth abruptly took the matter into her own hands.

"Wait here," she said as she headed for the door.

Briggs was a man of lightning fast reflexes; he had to be or he'd never have stayed alive all these years. But she took him so completely by surprise that for an instant he could do nothing. That was long enough for Elsabeth to vanish down the metal stairs.

Briggs cursed under his breath. He hoisted Sal over his shoulders in a fireman's carry, praying he wasn't hurting his friend further in the process, and followed her. Just what he needed to round out the day, the discovery that the woman he was passionately in love with had all the survival sense of your average fruit fly. God only knew what their children would be like.

Great time to be thinking about that. He had Sal to thank for the idea. Good ol' Sal. *Just get better, buddy, so I can tell you what I think of the godawful fix you worked us into.*

Elsabeth was near the foot of the stairs, partially hidden by a pillar. She frowned when she saw him. "Why didn't you wait?"

"Oh, right, like I'd really do that."

She sighed, accepting his bullheadedness. "I take it you want to make for the door over there?"

He shook his head. "I want the loading dock. That's where the van is. If we can get it, we'll be better off than on foot."

"That makes sense."

"I'm *so* glad you think so," he muttered caustically. "Look, just stay behind me, keep your head down, and—"

"Hold on a sec."

Elsabeth darted from behind the pillar. She stood, shoulders back, slender and poised, exactly as if she had stepped on stage. Her right arm lifted in a graceful arc.

The warehouse exploded—with sound, with color, with—Briggs was ready to swear this was true—primal vibrations surging up from the earth itself. Music poured out of empty space—ancient, fighting music reminiscent of gods and goddesses riding across a war-torn sky. The air filled with smoke, mauve and lavender smoke, but smoke all the same. A door slammed, men shouted, feet pounded. Chaos.

"Go!" Elsabeth yelled. They ran, heads down, through the smoke and the sound. Someone saw them and yelled, shouts rang out but they were gone, into the smoke, running faster and faster until they reached the loading dock where the black van still sat.

"Get in the back!" Briggs ordered. Elsabeth scrambled in and helped drag Sal in after her. She yanked the back doors closed as Briggs ran for the front. His hand felt for the ignition.

Nothing, no keys.

He shoved himself down between the front seat and the controls and felt for the metal panel he knew had to be there. It gave way with a metallic shriek. Inside was a maze of wires. Briggs reached unerringly for the two he wanted, shoved their tips together and heard the engine start.

He hit the automatic door control on the sunflap and gunned the motor. Men were pouring onto the loading dock, shouting, firing their weapons. In hard reverse, the van tore under the door, clearing it by inches, and out into the yard. Ahead lay the chain-link fence and the gate.

"Get down," Briggs yelled, "and hold on to Sal."

He pressed the accelerator flat, gripped the wheel hard and prayed. The van hit the gate flat-on and for an instant stalled, the wheels grinding. For heart-stopping moments nothing happened. The men were coming closer. Bullets winged the van. Elsabeth shut her eyes tight, her body shielding Sal. She whispered prayers she had learned in childhood—simple, desperate, heartfelt prayers. *Please, oh, please.* The only magic that really counted.

Three things happened more or less at once: the hinges cracked, the gate swayed, and the length of chain across it snapped.

They were through.

Chapter 15

The Bridgeport Hospital was a serious, no-nonsense facility devoted to the task of keeping people alive. It served a mixed clientele from the inner city, the outer suburbs, the nearby highway, the adjacent waterways and anywhere else human beings got hurt or sick. The staff there had seen everything not once but so many times that almost nothing seemed to ruffle them.

Except a wounded cop. That was in a category all by itself.

Briggs pulled the van up beside the emergency entrance. A security guard immediately began waving and shouting. "You can't park there, buddy. Gotta move it."

"We're bringing in a cop hurt bad on duty," Briggs said. The guard froze. He looked at Briggs hard, saw he was telling the truth, turned and ran for help. Briggs went around to the back of the van, yanked the door open, and lifted Sal out. Before he had taken two steps, they were engulfed.

"Outta the way," yelled a paramedic as he barreled through, pushing a stretcher. Half a dozen other medical personnel followed. A grim-faced young resident took one look at Sal and began shouting instructions that two equally grim nurses hurried to carry out. Before they were through the doors into the emergency room, Sal was on an IV, his blood pressure and heart were being monitored, and a blood sample had been taken and rushed off for typing.

The stretcher disappeared into a curtained treatment room. Briggs and Elsabeth stood staring after it. Before they could think very much about what was happening, a nurse took them in hand. She sat them down in a small cubicle, pulled out a clipboard, and let go with a series of rapid-fire questions.

What happened? Where? How long ago? Was he conscious? Where was he bleeding from? What kind of weapon was used? Fists? Something else? Previous injuries? Illnesses? Allergies? Was he on regular medication? Did he smoke? Drink? Do drugs?

"I don't know!" Briggs finally shouted, causing the woman to pull back slightly. "I didn't get there in time." The anger was gone from his voice. In its place there was only pain.

Elsabeth put herself between him and the nurse. Quietly but firmly she said, "We've told you all we can. You should call his wife."

"That's been taken care of," the nurse said, not unkindly. She looked once at Briggs, then added, "There's a cafeteria downstairs. It will be a while before we know anything. You might want to wait there.''

But Briggs had other ideas. ''I need a drink,'' he said. They walked across the street to a bar that had seen better days but still had a homey seediness about it. Elsabeth asked for a glass of mineral water. Briggs ordered scotch. When it came, he drank it down in a single swallow.

''God, I hate the taste of that stuff,'' he said.

Elsabeth did not ask him why he drank it then. She knew that he didn't, not typically. She knew a great deal about him, considering the short time they had actually been together. But it was like that sometimes. She accepted the gift of such knowledge humbly, knowing better than to question it. Like life itself, it simply was.

''Do you want to go back?'' she asked.

He nodded. ''I have to know.''

The emergency room was even more crowded when they returned. Men in blue uniforms stood around talking quietly with each other. Other men in suits and sport jackets walked up and down in the hallway. They all knew Briggs, they all greeted him cordially. In their eyes was not speculation, as Elsabeth had half expected, but respect and affection. Technically Briggs was off the force, but in reality these men still considered him one of their own.

One of the plainclothes detectives came up to them. He nodded to Elsabeth before turning his attention to Briggs. ''Sal's in the OR. He's got some busted ribs, a collapsed lung, a concussion, and they're pretty sure his spleen's gonna have to come out. Mrs. D'Angelo's on her way here along with a couple of their sons. I'd like to be able to tell her we know who did this."

Briggs hesitated. Quietly he said, "Where's Leary?"

"I've got no idea. What's he got to do with this?"

"What about Stevens, the federal guy?"

"Ditto. You wanna tell me what's going on?"

Briggs sighed. He took a deep breath. "Let's sit down."

They sat.

Briggs talked.

He spoke for a long time. The detective interrupted with a couple of questions. About halfway through, he called several other men over. They had questions, too, though not many. Mostly they just scowled.

Elsabeth excused herself and went to the ladies' room. She spent as much time in there as she decently could, splashing cold water on her face and brushing her hair with her fingers. She'd remembered her basic magic equipment—the stuff she was never without—but she didn't have a comb. She'd found her pocket-book in the back of the van when she and Briggs hi-jacked it. That had been a big relief since Martha Byrnes's book was in it. No comb, though, no lip-stick, not even a hankie. Georgette would not have been pleased.

She sighed, thinking of the days of her childhood when ladies' rooms had been supplied with vending machines that sold all manner of useful things, not merely combs but plastic hair protectors, packets of tissues, bits of costume jewelry and the sort. There had been special machines that provided squirts of per-fume for a dime.

Not anymore. The only vending machines she saw in this ladies' room sold articles of a far more elementary nature. She supposed that was for the best. Women were less protected now and less restricted. Which didn't change the fact that she'd been damn glad to see Briggs.

She looked at herself in the mirror, hardly noticing how pale she was. Her eyes looked like dark, limpid pools, her lips were swollen, and her hair—the less said about it the better. If Briggs hadn't gotten there, she'd be dead right now or close to it. Chumpster and the others had made their plans quite clear. She tried a fierce look in the mirror, decided it didn't wash and went back into the corridor.

He was sitting alone, his head in his hands. She forced herself to walk slowly. Silently she sat down beside him.

"What now?" she asked.

"The rule book, that's what."

"What does that mean?"

"It means the D.A. is informed of what happened and he makes a decision about what to do next. Chumpster, Ruglio and the Stick—he's out, too—should never have been released on bail. It looks as if they were let out deliberately so Stevens and Leary could keep the ball in play. They were still using the two of us as bait, hoping to reel in Hodding. They blew that but what happens next is anybody's guess. The D.A. may choose to intervene directly and stop them or he may choose to go along. Whatever he decides, it's not going to be until tomorrow at the earliest."

"So we stay?"

He shook his head and stood up. "No, we go. We're not doing Sal any good here and we both need some rest. We'll use my place."

"Excuse me, but that's where I got clonked on the head by the bad guys. I'm not exactly eager to go back there."

"Donnelly, that's the guy who told us about Sal, is sending a detail over. We'll be fine. Better, in fact, than anywhere else."

"What's wrong with my house?" she asked.

"It's farther away, for one thing. Also, Stevens has a guy there."

"We'll get rid of him. I want to sleep in my own bed." She looked at him pointedly. When he grinned, she sniffed and looked away. "Also, I want my cat back."

"Oh, yeah, let's not forget Zared. Heaven only knows how this will have affected his delicate psyche."

"Forget his psyche, I'm talking about mine. Seriously, if the guy Stevens sent over is still dumb enough to be there, I'll take care of him."

Briggs laughed. For a moment he looked younger and almost carefree. "The rabbit thing again?"

"You think I'm kidding."

He gave her a disconcerting look. "Actually, I'm not sure. Let me call ahead and at least give the guy a fighting chance."

"Sissy," Elsabeth murmured.

"What was that?"

"You heard me."

"Hold the thought, sweetie. We'll *discuss* it later."

He called. The phone rang three times before Elsabeth's answering machine clicked on. When her message had run through and the tone had sounded, Briggs offered the tape some short, explicit advice.

"That ought to do it," he said as he hung up.

"You think so?"

He took her arm. "Let's find out."

"I'm surprised," she said when they were back out on the street in front of the hospital. "I thought you'd hold out more for your place."

He shrugged. "I like your house better."

"Even though it's in the boonies?"

"Yeah, even though."

The van was still parked near the emergency entrance but it was guarded by a couple of steely eyed cops who, though they nodded cordially enough to Briggs, didn't look like they'd take any nonsense.

"Where's the M.G.?" Elsabeth asked.

"A couple of blocks from the warehouse." He stuck a hand in his pants pocket, searching for change.

She rolled her eyes. "The bus again."

"Hey, with me you only go first class. We'll take a cab."

Zared was glad to see them. He fussed dreadfully, rubbing up against their ankles, kneading his paws ecstatically, threatening to crack the plaster with his purrs.

"He hasn't been eating," Mrs. Cavendish confessed. "I poached some chicken for him this morning but he wouldn't touch it."

Elsabeth picked him up. He did feel lighter. She accepted the guilt, knowing she had no choice. Zared would insist on it.

"He'll be fine now. Thank you so much for looking after him."

Mrs. Cavendish saw them off with a relieved wave. They crossed the road to the house, which was satisfyingly vacant. Stevens's man had gotten the message. He was gone without a trace.

In the kitchen Elsabeth opened up a can of sardines, spooned it into a bowl and stepped back just in time to avoid being trampled by Zared. Still purring, he wolfed the meal down and looked at her expectantly.

"I thought cats were fastidious," Briggs said. "Picky, even."

She laughed and opened another can. "It's good to be home."

Briggs sighed. She really loved the old place. So he'd sell the condo. Even in the presently tight real estate market, waterfront properties were always popular. Besides, it had never been more to him than somewhere to sleep.

With Zared properly seen to, she was free to fix dinner for the humans. Briggs sat on a stool at the counter and watched her. He waited until she'd gotten the tomatoes sliced before he said, "So you want to tell me what you did at the warehouse?"

She rinsed the razor-sharp knife off and looked at him innocently. "What do you mean?"

"Come on. The music—what was that, Wagner's *Ride of the Valkyries?*—and all the rest of it. I thought we were standing smack on top of the San Andreas Fault just in time for the big one. Don't tell me that was done with props."

Elsabeth frowned. She took out a package of skinned and boned chicken breasts, picked up a mallet and began pounding them purposefully. "The music came from a portable tape deck I happened to find in the office. The smoke was my usual. There were no vibrations."

"No vi—" He broke off, looking at her. He'd felt them, he knew he had.

Or had he?

"How would I make vibrations?" she asked. "Be sensible. That's impossible." She spoke very firmly, refusing to entertain any alternative. She herself had not felt any vibrations, of that she was certain. But then she had been very busy. Over the years there had been a few occasions when in the midst of a routine she had practiced hundreds of times something would suddenly...what? There weren't really any words for it. *Shift* was the closest she could come. Something would shift and she would have a sense of standing outside herself, free of all the usual restrictions. Free to do anything her imagination could conjure.

But that was crazy, not to mention frightening. It was better not to dwell on such things.

"What about the smoke?" Briggs asked, not convinced yet. What he'd seen just now in her face made him wonder all the more. "You just happened to have all your equipment with you?"

"It doesn't take much. Besides, I always carry *some* props. It's a habit."

He supposed that was true. Anyway, it made sense. It was certainly simpler than anything he could think of.

"We got lucky," he said.

She nodded. "Maybe more than that. I don't know about you, but I was praying awfully hard."

He popped a peanut in his mouth, chewed reflectively and said, "That reminds me, you want a church wedding?"

Elsabeth gave the chicken one more really good whack, put down the mallet and said, "If that was supposed to be a proposal, you should know that on a romance scale of one to ten, it's a minus twenty. Maybe even a thirty."

Briggs flushed. The phenomenon was so unexpected that it took her completely aback. "It's okay," she said. "I don't expect hearts and flowers."

"But you ought to have them. I'm just no good at that part. The fact is I'm kind of nervous at the moment."

"How come?"

"You *could* say no," he reminded her.

"Oh." She'd forgotten about that. The mere possibility of refusing to marry him seemed outlandish, comical even. "Why would I want to do that?"

"I can't imagine. I mean, you've got to admit I know how to show you a good time. First, you got terrorized by a backfire during our great fishing expedition, then two guys break in here, then you get hit over the head and hauled off to one of Bridgeport's finer warehouses, then you get to spend a really neat afternoon sitting around an emergency room, then..."

She shrugged. "I've been through worse."

Briggs looked startled. It wasn't as good as actually seeing him blush but it wasn't bad, either.

"Besides," she added, "you forgot Toucarow, New Hampshire's hot spot."

"Yeah, Toucarow." Their eyes met. Unspoken between them were memories of exactly what had transpired in their cabin. All things considered, it was amazing it was still standing.

Elsabeth cleared her throat. "Maybe we could go back there someday."

"Okay with me. About church and the, uh, you know—"

"Wedding?"

"Yeah, that. First time I got married it was at city hall. I'd like to do it up right this time."

Elsabeth made a mental note: definitely a church wedding *with* all of the trimmings. Her years on the hotel tour had left her with a grab bag of useful names. She knew exactly who to go to for great ice sculptures, fantastic hors d'oeuvres, honest open bars, really good music, the whole bit. A few phone calls and they'd be all set.

Wait a minute, what was she thinking? He was talking about marriage, till death do us part, the whole nine yards. *Commitment.*

"How do you like kids?" he asked, as though it was the kind of question she got asked every day.

"Fried," she said. At his surprised look she explained hastily. "W.C. Fields always said that. It's a great line."

He drew back reprovingly. "I'm trying to be serious here."

"I am, too," Elsabeth said. "I am seriously terrified."

"What of?"

"Not of you," she said hastily. "You're—" She broke off, searching for a word that was accurate without being adolescently extravagant. Her eyes softened in a smile. "Wonderful."

He grinned back at her. "Good, I was getting worried there. You're scared of getting married." When she nodded, he said, "That's normal."

"Why don't we have dinner and talk about this later?" she suggested, sounding very sensible. She managed that so rarely that it startled her. She almost dropped the mallet.

He shrugged. "Okay. Want me to do anything?"

Just sit there forever and ever, looking gorgeous and fantastic, the kind of man every woman dreams of and too few ever find.

"No, thanks, I've got everything under control."

And pigs fly. If she kept this up, her nose would start growing. "This chicken is going to take a while. If it doesn't cook slowly, it'll be tough."

"Is this a group project or can it be trusted on its own?"

"Actually, chicken does far better left unobserved, much like a pot of water put on to boil," she said airily.

"Speaking of coming to a boil..."

She shook her head. "That's terrible, you can do better than that."

He stood up and held out a hand to her. "I'm the strong, silent type, remember?"

* * *

The quiet bedroom under the eaves received them gently. They came into each other's arms with the hunger of lovers who have been years apart, not mere hours.

Swiftly, his eyes holding hers, Briggs undid the two big buttons that held the straps of Elsabeth's overalls. The front dropped forward. Beneath it she wore a loose cotton T-shirt. He slid his hands beneath the fabric, feeling the smooth warmth of her back interrupted only by the band of her bra. A subtle, elusive fragrance rose to tantalize him. She smelled of flowers, wind and sun. He breathed in again deeply and let the scent fill him.

Her head tipped back, spilling the luxuriant fall of her hair halfway down her back. It teased his wrists as he eased the T-shirt off her. His fingers brushed lightly over her breasts before coming to rest on the front closing of the bra. He undid it, letting the thin lace part without removing it entirely. Her breasts were full and firm. They spilled out to be received into his palms. Gently his thumbs rubbed back and forth over the nipples. He waited until she moaned softly before he bent his head and took her into his mouth.

Elsabeth's back arched. The rough velvet of his unshaven cheeks abraded her lightly even as the sucking motion of his mouth sent reverberations deep into her womb. Tremors of pleasure crested within her. By the time he raised his head again, her eyes were deep and slumberous with passion.

"Undress me," he said quietly. The tip of her tongue moistened her lips. She raised her hands, pale and slender in the dim light, and did as he said.

He had taken the denim jacket off when they got to the house, and the gun was already on the table beside the bed. She fumbled slightly as she undid the buttons of his shirt and eased it off. His chest was broad, lightly furred with springy dark hair and burnished by the sun. She managed to unfasten the buckle of his leather belt and undo the snap of his jeans. The zipper slid down an inch, another. She could feel the hard heat of him move against her hand.

"Don't stop," he rasped.

Breathing raggedly, she pulled the zipper the rest of the way down. Briggs sat on the edge of the bed and yanked his shoes off. The jeans followed. Dressed only in briefs, he pulled her to him, cradling her between the arc of his thighs. The heat and strength of him engulfed her. She was barely able to stand and had to brace her hands against his powerful shoulders.

He smiled as his mouth claimed hers, his tongue plunging deeply. At the same time he slipped the lacy panties from her. They fell together onto the bed. Elsabeth cried out as his hands moved, finding the warm, wet cleft. His fingers caressed her boldly, driving her closer and closer to the edge.

Abruptly he moved. "Finish it," he said.

For a moment she didn't understand what he meant. When she did, she blushed. She reached out, touched the elastic band at the top of his briefs and slowly pulled them off.

His manhood sprang free, rising long and hard from the nest of curls at his groin. Before she could speak or move, he lifted her around the hips. Slowly, inch by inch, he lowered her onto him.

So great was Elsabeth's arousal that her pleasure began to peak almost immediately. Her head back, the vein in her neck showing blue against the pale translucence of her skin, she cried out his name. Shuddering tremors seized her. She clung to him as the world dissolved—room, bed, bodies, all vanishing with it. There was only love, and each other, and the certain knowledge that this was how they were always meant to be.

Afterward she snuggled close in his arms, warm and safe. Briggs stroked her hair gently as she listened to the beat of his heart beneath her cheek. When he touched his lips lightly to her forehead, her mouth curved in a smile.

"This is so..." she began, fumbling for the word.

"So what?" he asked.

"I don't know exactly." She shifted slightly so that she could look at him. "Nice certainly doesn't cover it. Great's better but it's been overused. Scary's part of it but for sure not all."

"Scary? Why?"

"All the giving... and receiving... not being really separate anymore..." She broke off, embarrassed by the intensity of her own feelings. "I'm not doing this very well. You're the writer, you tell me."

He laughed gently and tightened his arms around her. "Are you kidding? People have been trying to do that ever since the first fool picked up the first stick and started scratching marks in the dirt. They'll still be doing it on the last day of the last year before the sun goes nova or whatever happens to end it all." He tucked her closer and rested his head on top of hers.

"Words are fine for most things. For this you need something more basic."

"Like what?" Elsabeth asked.

He showed her.

Chapter 16

Early the next morning, while Elsabeth was still asleep, Briggs went outside to talk with the surveillance team Donnelly had deployed. The two young officers didn't seem to mind too much that he'd gone up to Redding instead of to his condo. It was all the same so far as they were concerned.

"Nothing moving," the shorter of the two said. "Absolutely nothing. This place is deader than dead."

"Sure is," his partner agreed. "Kinda pretty, though."

"What's the word on Lieutenant D'Angelo?" Briggs asked.

"He came through the surgery real good. They had him in intensive care overnight but they were moving him into his own room this morning. Also, 'round about midnight a wino trying to catch a few winks down near the water saw something funny floating by.

Turned out to be our old buddy, Dan Ruglio, or what was left of him.''

Briggs frowned. ''Anything on the other two?''

The young officer shook his head. ''Not so far as we've heard. After almost killing a cop, they've got to be on the run. But they won't get far.''

Briggs wished he shared the same confidence. The fact that Ruglio was dead and the other two were missing worried him. Had they killed the other man or had someone else done it for them?

Whichever was the case, he wasn't going to find the answer in Redding. The moment he and Elsabeth were dressed, they headed for the hospital. As the officers had said, Sal had been moved to a private room. A policeman stood outside his door while several others watched the building entrances. No one was taking any chances.

Mrs. D'Angelo was there with her husband. She was a slender, dark-haired woman with lively features and a gentle manner. The events of the past few hours had left their mark on her but she seemed to be coming back fast. Certainly the smile she gave them indicated that.

''Briggs,'' she said, holding out a hand. ''I'm so glad you're here. What you did . . . there's just no way to thank you enough.''

Briggs shrugged and looked embarrassed. ''I didn't do much, Maria, certainly nothing Sal wouldn't have done for me.''

Sal laughed, winced as the effort hurt his sides, and held out his own hand. He was still hooked up to an IV and various monitors. His head was swathed in bandages as was his chest. Beneath the smile, his complexion was gray.

"I acted like a dope," he said apologetically, "going in there on my own. I should have gotten Donnelly and some of the other guys to go along. But with Leary and Stevens acting so weird, and careers maybe on the line, it didn't seem right to involve anyone else."

"What about those two?" Briggs asked, glad to move away from the subject of their gratitude.

Sal's smile vanished. He looked very tough all of a sudden. "Leary's on leave of absence while the D.A. decides what to do with him. Stevens is back in Washington cooling his heels while somebody decides whether or not to let him resign quietly." He started to laugh, winced again and thought better of it. "Thank God the two of them aren't typical or we'd all be in a hell of a lot more trouble than we are."

"I know how Leary got into this," Briggs said, "but what brought Stevens in?"

"Leary heard a rumor the Feds were after Hodding," Sal said. "When the info turned up on the warehouse linking Hodding to Dickinson's murder, he decided to see how much mileage he could get outta it. Stevens was the guy running the investigation on Hodding so the two of them teamed up. The bottom line is neither of them was convinced a jury would believe Chumpster and the others when they said Hodding ordered Dickinson's murder. The kind of legal heat Hodding can afford just made that too dicey. Leary and Stevens cooked up the scheme to put them back on the street, hoping that would cause Hodding to do something to incriminate himself. Never mind prosecuting Chumpster and the others for Dickinson's murder or the attack on you, that was small potatoes. Only Hodding mattered to them. It was a real stupid idea but it's the kind of thing people come up with when all they're thinking about is their own careers.''

"So, where does all this leave us with Hodding?" Briggs asked.

Sal sighed. He averted his eyes for a moment before he said, "You're not going to like this pal, but that end of it hasn't changed. There's still no evidence to tie Hodding to the Dickinson killing, or to the attempts on the two of you."

"Who's Hodding?" Elsabeth asked.

Briefly Briggs told her. When he finished she said, "If he owns the warehouse where we were held, isn't that a link?"

Sal shook his head regretfully. "It's owned by a company that's owned by a company that's owned by... and so on. Hodding will claim he had no idea what was going on there and there's nothing to prove him wrong."

"Are you trying to tell me," Elsabeth asked, "that this whole thing could turn out to be an exercise in futility? This Hodding person gets away with having Dickinson killed, scaring the living daylights out of me, hurting you and God only knows what else?"

"Nobody wants that to happen," Sal said, "but there's only so much we can do."

"I hate to say this," Elsabeth told them, "but I'm beginning to understand how Stevens and Leary came up with this crazy scheme. If Hodding is half as bad as you say he is, they must be going nuts trying to get him."

"That's about the size of it," Sal agreed. "There's an awful lot of frustration built into this job. Briggs can tell you that."

Briggs had been staring out the window through much of this. Now he turned back to them. He looked distracted. Absently he said, "Sure, Sal. Listen, I'm really glad you're on the mend. When they let you out of here, we're going to take you and Maria out to celebrate. But in the meantime, you need to get some rest."

He took Elsabeth's arm and headed toward the door. "Maria, if you need anything, you call us right away."

"Sure," she murmured, looking surprised, "sure, Briggs."

"Hey, wait a minute," Sal said. "What's the rush? You just got here."

"We'll be back, buddy," Briggs said gently.

Sal looked from him to Elsabeth, his brows together. "You make sure of that, pal. You make damn sure of it. No crazy stuff. Remember, you're a civilian now."

When they were outside in the corridor, walking past the banks of rooms on their way to the elevators, Elsabeth asked, "Why did he think he needed to remind you of that?"

"Who knows? Sal always did have a great imagination."

She made a noncommittal sound and got into the elevator. They rode down to the main floor and were getting off when Briggs said, "I'll drive you home, then I've got some business to take care of."

"Doing what, hunting down Hodding?" When he continued to look at her as though she were speaking some unknown tongue, she said, "You never returned Sal's gun, did you? Maybe he was too doped up to notice but I wasn't. What are you planning to do, walk up to his front door, tell him who you are and listen while he confesses?"

"Don't be crazy. Come on, we're going home."

Elsabeth stood her ground, her fists clenched and her eyes shooting fire. "You're not getting the message, Briggs. I'm not going anywhere without you. I don't like this business with Hodding any more than you do, but I'm smart enough to know you can't handle it on your own. Nobody can."

He took firm hold of his patience and drew her off to one side of the lobby. "Look, there's something you're *not* getting. Whatever happens with Chumpster and the Stick, Hodding knows you can tie them to Dickinson's killing. That means as long as you're around they've got every reason to cut themselves a deal even if that means selling him out. But if you're not around, Hodding can make it worth their while to do the time for the attack on Sal. Even though Sal's a cop, they probably wouldn't get more than ten to fifteen years. With time off for good behavior, they could be out in five. Hodding could guarantee them a million dollars for every year they do and it wouldn't dent him any."

He took a deep breath and concluded, "While he's on the loose, your life is on the line."

For Briggs, that was a long speech but it made his point. However, it didn't change Elsabeth's mind. If anything, it made her more determined than ever.

"I'm going with you."

"Like hell."

She smiled sweetly. "If I don't, I'll go on my own."

The look that crossed his face was forbidding. It was almost enough to make her back down. Almost, but not quite. She looked at him unflinchingly. "People like Hodding have to be stopped. You know that, I know that. If he's not, he goes on selling weapons and screwing up the world. And I spend the rest of my life looking over my shoulder. No, thanks."

"So what exactly are you suggesting?" Briggs demanded.

She took a deep breath, took a firm grip on her courage and said, "I'm suggesting we pay Mr. Hodding a visit." Quickly, before he could refuse again, she added, "I can help, Briggs, you know I can. You saw what I can do back at the warehouse. Between us, we'll have a real shot at him."

Her choice of words gave Briggs pause. "Understand, I'm talking about bringing him in alive."

Elsabeth's eyes widened. She hadn't considered any other alternative. "I wouldn't...that is, I'd never..."

"Okay," Briggs said, holding up a hand, "just so we understand each other. Make sure you also understand this—I'm agreeing only because I know you are stubborn enough to go off on your own if I don't. That much I've figured out. But you will do *exactly* what I tell you to do. We'll go by his place, see how things look, but that's all. Got it?"

Elsabeth nodded. She was trying hard to contain her excitement but didn't succeed. Briggs shot her a reproving glance as they got into the car.

"I'm serious," he said. "This is not some little jaunt we're going on. You'll do what you're told."

"Don't I always?" Elsabeth asked with a grin.

He sighed. "Now I see what I'm letting myself in for, heaven help me."

They both knew he wasn't talking about the visit to Hodding. He had something a lot more permanent in mind.

Elsabeth shot him a sidelong glance. "Having second thoughts?"

She held her breath until he said, "Sure, aren't you? Everybody has second thoughts, and third and fourth thoughts, too. So what? They don't change anything."

She smiled and settled back in the seat. But she was far from being as calm as she looked. What were they going to do, drive right up to Hodding's place and ring the bell?

Not if the direction they were going in was any indication. Briggs seemed to be headed for his condo.

"Want to tell me the game plan?" she asked.

He didn't but she'd worm it out of him anyway, so he went ahead.

"I did a little research. Hodding is giving a big bash tonight, some kind of a charity ball. We're going."

"He invited us? How nice."

"Cute. We're crashing."

"Front door or back?"

His eyebrows rose. "Sounds like you've done this kind of thing before."

"Once or twice in my young and feckless days."

"When was that, last week?"

"Cute. Which way?"

"Front door."

"That means we have to dress."

"Which is why we're going to my place. I've got to pick up my tux."

Her eyebrows rose. "La-di-da. Don't most guys just rent them?"

"I bought it for an undercover job I was on," he explained. "What about you, you have anything to wear?"

"How about my tux?"

"I'm letting you out right here."

"Okay," she said, laughing. "Yes, I have something to wear. Feel better?"

"Loads."

An hour later they were back at Elsabeth's house. She left Briggs to fend for himself and went upstairs to soak in a bubble bath. That done, she dried and powdered herself, brushed her hair a hundred strokes and got down to the serious business of preparing for a fancy charity bash in Greenwich. She'd entertained at a few such functions herself but this was the first time she'd be attending as a guest. Well, sort of as a guest. Gate-crasher had such a harsh ring to it.

Fortunately she had the perfect dress, one she'd bought in a weak moment and never before had occasion to wear. Elsabeth had a weakness for "antique" clothes, especially those from the 1930s and 1940s. At one time such garments could be had for a song at tag sales and in junk shops. No more. Now they were sold in boutiques for prices that would have caused the original owners to gag.

Still, she thought as she took the dress from its padded hanger and held it in front of her, it was worth it. The material was satin, the kind that was all but unavailable today except in the most expensive couturier originals. The sheer weight of it was enough to make her feel languorous and indulged. The color was black, not a deep murky black but a black that seemed to have swallowed moonlight. Only by holding the material directly up to the eye was it possible to see the infinitesimal threads of silver woven into the cloth. The bodice, what there was of it, was tightly fitted. It hugged Elsabeth's small waist and the swell of her breasts. Tiny strips of bone held the bodice up but it appeared to be suspended by no more than good intentions and her own endowments. The skirt was bell-shaped, falling to midcalf with a rustling petticoat beneath. When she turned, it ballooned around her like the blossom of a midnight flower. The fabric and the color made her skin look even paler than usual and emphasized the fiery glory of her hair tumbling over her shoulders in almost wild disarray. Lastly, she touched that most classic of perfumes, Chanel No. 5, to her wrists and the cleft between her breasts. On a cloud of bygone femininity, she floated from the room and down the stairs to where Briggs awaited.

She got almost to the last step before she stopped and simply stared. He was standing in the living room in the tuxedo he had apparently been born to wear. Gone was the rough-edged street cop. In his place was a masterfully elegant man of grace and strength that left her breathless.

So much so that she barely noticed the look of surprise that darted through his eyes. He started to say something, stopped and tried again.

"You look—beautiful."

"Thank you," she said gravely. "You look quite the thing yourself."

He smiled and inclined his head. "I guess we both clean up pretty good."

She held out her hand, glad that the Briggs she knew hadn't disappeared entirely. Behind those slumberous eyes, his sense of humor was still intact.

"Shall we?" she asked.

Even the old M.G. seemed to suit their attire and their mood. The engine purred, the wheels spun, and all too soon they were in Greenwich. They got off the interstate in the downtown area and headed north. Elsabeth knew the town fairly well. She liked it for shopping, the occasional dinner out or just wandering around on a weekend afternoon. Despite all the building that had gone on, many of the old houses had survived. There was still a lot of history in Greenwich. Also, *a lot* of money.

She said as much to Briggs. "That's what this place is all about," he said. "There are basically three kinds of people here—old money, new money and no money. The first two aren't hard to find, the last almost extinct."

"I suppose Hodding's new money," Elsabeth said.

"Not really. He came from a very wealthy family that fell on hard times. They were down to their last million or two when Hod decided he needed a better way to put caviar on the table. Guns, and everything that goes with them, proved to be it."

"He has no conscience at all?"

Briggs laughed, a harsh sound in the small car. "You've got to be kidding."

They left it at that. On either side of them, the smaller mansions of Greenwich flowed past. Set on a couple of acres, many recently built and bought with yuppie money in the rah-rah 1980s, they were overstuffed reminders of an age of excess. Further on, where the road grew narrower, houses became sparser. Now instead of one every few acres, they drove for long stretches without seeing any sign of life. This was "back-country" Greenwich, home to the really serious money—old or new.

They passed horse farms framed by vast expanses of rolling lawn dotted with white fences that might have come straight out of bluegrass Kentucky. There were barns and stables worth more than most people's homes, immense ponds where swans drifted among imported lily pads, and, here and there, almost hidden behind the screens of Italian poplars, there were houses. Most of them had been built long ago and were lovingly maintained. They dated from an age of cheap servants, no income tax, and little inhibition. An age when the pursuit of luxury could consume an entire lifetime without ever being satisfied—or questioned.

Elsabeth's eyes darkened. She had no objection to people living well, even luxuriously. But the arms merchant paid his way with other people's lives. That she could not accept.

"How much farther?" she asked.

"Not far." They rounded a corner and came onto a stretch of road bordered on either side by a high stone wall. The wall ran for at least a quarter mile before it was interrupted on one side by a high, wrought-iron gate that stood open. Floodlights illuminated the road leading beyond it. Several cars—a Rolls and two Jaguars among them—were ahead of them, giving them a chance to survey what they could of the weapon dealer's estate.

"It's huge," Elsabeth said.

"One hundred and twenty acres," Briggs said. "The house was finished in 1921. It contains thirty-seven rooms. There are also half a dozen or so outbuildings. Stonemasons imported from Europe worked more than three years to construct it all. The original owner was a bootlegger who made it big smuggling hooch during Prohibition. Hodding bought it five years ago." He rattled off the facts while eyeing the gate. Old Hod didn't seem to bother with much in the way of security but looks could be deceptive.

"So this isn't the family manse he was desperate to hold on to?"

"Not by a long shot. Even in their best days, they were small potatoes compared to this."

"Isn't it nice that he's come up in the world."

The road ahead cleared. They passed through the gates and continued on in the line of cars approaching the house. A quarter mile later, it came into view. The original owner had apparently had a fondness for French châteaus, enough to construct one three thousand miles away from where it should have been. The facade stretched several hundred feet in either direction from the entrance. Three stories of gray stone rose to a gabled roof set off by fanciful turrets. Dozens of windows shone with light. Music poured from the open French doors that lined the balustrade and from the main entrance through which elegantly dressed men and women were proceeding.

A valet stood ready to park the car. Briggs slipped him a twenty and said, "Keep her near the front with the keys in the ignition."

The man nodded, palmed the tip and jumped behind the wheel. Briggs winced as the tires squealed.

"It's okay," Elsabeth said soothingly. She lifted her skirt and together they climbed the half dozen steps. At the top were two burly young men who looked highly uncomfortable in formal dress. They were checking invitations.

Immediately ahead of Briggs and Elsabeth was an elderly couple, both silver-haired and distinguished. The gentleman was having trouble remembering where he'd put their invitation. Briggs came up directly behind them. He smiled sympathetically at their predicament and began patting his own pockets as though the missing item might be in one of them.

"Maybe I've got it," he said with an apologetic nod to the security man.

The older gentleman gave him a puzzled look but was too absorbed in his search to notice much else. Beside him, his wife tapped her foot impatiently.

"Really, Reginald," she said, "this sort of thing happens all the time."

"Can't understand why, my dear," he murmured. "I distinctly told Devonshire to make sure the invitation was in my trouser pocket. The old blighter used to be so reliable, but now—"

"He's no older than you are, Reginald. You mustn't try to use age as an excuse."

"I really think it may be my fault," Briggs said. He turned to Elsabeth. "Darling, I didn't give it to you, by any chance?"

She shook her head and moved a little closer to the elderly woman.

"Aha!" the old gentleman said. With a flourish he withdrew an embossed and engraved card, and presented it to the guard. "Knew I had it. Old Devonshire has never let me down. Isn't that right, dear?"

"Absolutely," Elsabeth said. She smiled brightly and took Briggs's arm. Together with the older couple they strolled into the entry hall. Elsabeth held her breath for a moment, wondering if the guard would examine the invitation closely enough to see that it was only for two people. But they had timed their arrival well. The press of guests directly behind them prevented him from giving it anything more than a cursory glance.

Once inside, they parted swiftly from the older couple before questions could be asked and made their way directly to the back of the room where a string quartet was playing. Briggs took two fluted glasses of champagne off the tray of a passing waiter and handed one to Elsabeth.

"So far so good," he said.

"Here's mud in your eye." She took a sip of the crisp, dry champagne and scanned the room. More than a hundred guests were on hand already and the stream through the door showed no sign of ebbing. The noise level was high and promised to go higher. Light gleamed off what would have been an emper-

or's ransom in jewels had they been real. Elsabeth suspected most of them weren't, even in this crowd. Insurance premiums being what they were, most of the genuine stuff never saw the outside of a vault. But the display was impressive all the same. As were the myriad swirling colors of the evening gowns and the heady scent of perfumes drifting on the evening air.

She closed her eyes for a moment, feeling disoriented. It was almost impossible to believe that so much beauty and pleasure could be brought together in a place ruled by death.

When she opened her eyes her gaze settled on a tall, well-built man. He stood at the center of a cluster of people yet he seemed to hold himself somewhat aloof. Fair-haired, lightly tanned with aristocratic features, he was easily one of the handsomest men Elsabeth had ever seen. But his looks left her completely cold. There was something about him, a certain blankness in his eyes, a twist of cruelty in his mouth that sent a shiver of dislike through her.

Still looking at him, she said, "That's Hodding, isn't it?"

Briggs looked in the same direction and nodded. He took her glass and set it down with his own. His hand grasped hers reassuringly as he said, "We're on, sweetheart."

Chapter 17

The plan was as simple as it was dangerous—to give the house as thorough a go-through as they could manage in the hope of turning up something incriminating that would enable the police to get a search warrant. The chances of success were slim, but Hodding's recent actions—killing Dickinson, the break-in at Elsabeth's house, Ruglio's demise—all suggested he was getting overly confident. Or perhaps desperate. Men who were desperate tended to be careless.

The problem was where to begin. The house was immense. It was filled with corridors that seemed to wander off into nowhere, three floors of rooms plus basements and attics, and all of it was protected by unknown security measures.

"Begin at the beginning," Georgette had always said, which wasn't in the least original but did have the virtue of being irrefutable.

They started in the gallery that ran behind the entry hall, walking down it hand in hand like guests who merely sought a few moments of tranquility while admiring their host's art collection. The gallery took them to the library, a huge baroque room with a vaulted ceiling, walls lined with bookcases, priceless Oriental rugs on the parquet floor and a fireplace ideal for roasting ox. The bookcases were crammed with books, thousands of them, all with brightly hued leather bindings and gold-etched lettering.

Elsabeth took one of the volumes down and examined it to satisfy her curiosity. "Just as I thought, the pages have never been cut."

Briggs glanced up from the desk he'd been scrutinizing. "What's that?"

"The books, they're reproductions of books printed hundreds of years ago, even down to the uncut pages. Hodding's never touched them." She shook her head sadly, thinking of the awful waste. "He doesn't read."

"I could have told you that. He went to one of the finest prep schools in the country and a top Ivy League college but his idea of a good time is snorting a few lines of coke with his pals while they decide what country to screw up next."

"Charming."

Briggs shrugged. The desk proved useless. Most of the drawers were empty and the only contents he did find were sheets of unused notepaper with Hodding's name and address elaborately engraved on the letterhead.

The other rooms on the first floor proved equally unhelpful. The drawing room was filled with Chinese antiques that made Elsabeth's eyes light up but again there was nothing remotely personal. The same was true of the music room, the morning room, the baronial dining room that comfortably sat sixty, the ballroom, and so on. They might as well have been wandering through a stage set for all the insight provided into the man who supposedly lived there.

"This is getting weird," Elsabeth said when they paused for a break. She nibbled a sliver of toasted bread spread with pâté and tried to put her finger on what was bothering her.

"I've been in places where the decorator had obviously had too much influence, but never quite like this. There isn't a magazine, a real book, a television set, a stereo, not even a coaster, for heaven's sake. Nothing to suggest this house is actually used."

"He lives here at least six months out of every year," Briggs said. "His dossier makes that clear. Somewhere there's got to be something personal."

They eyed each other. Elsabeth spoke first. "Upstairs."

"We can explain wandering around down here," Briggs reminded her. "After that, it gets dicier."

"There are a lot of people here tonight," Elsabeth said. "Including a lot of ladies drinking a lot of champagne. It's not impossible somebody would go looking for a bathroom upstairs."

"Okay," Briggs said reluctantly. "But remember what I said, you do what I say. No arguments, no delays, got it?"

"Got it."

He looked at her rather dubiously but allowed her to lead the way up the winding marble staircase to the second floor.

Several other couples had gotten there ahead of them and not always on as innocent an errand as Elsabeth had suggested. Amorous embraces were the least of it. Briggs had to remember that he was no longer a law officer and could not automatically arrest users of illicit drugs.

That realization did nothing to improve his mood. He scowled darkly, frightening several people who happened to be passing by.

"Behave yourself," Elsabeth murmured.

He tried, but the anger was there and growing. Sensing it, Elsabeth said, "Come on, we've got work to do."

The corridor ahead of them was framed by doors, most of them undoubtedly leading to bedrooms. She put her hand on the first knob, only to be stopped by Briggs. He smiled gently. "Better let me go first."

She looked puzzled for a moment before understanding dawned. There was no reason to think the amorous embraces were confined to the hallway.

The first bedroom was empty, as was the second. In the third, the bed had been used but was presently empty. The fourth was not.

Briggs shut the door hastily. He looked bemused. "Must be a gymnast."

"What?"

"The woman, she must be a gymnast."

Elsabeth blushed. "I don't want to know."

He laughed and moved on down the hall. At the end of the corridor on a corner of the building, they came to what was apparently Hodding's personal suite. Any of the more megalomaniacal French kings would have been perfectly at home there. Velvet curtains hung at the floor-to-ceiling windows. An oversized canopy bed set on a dais held pride of place. Apart from it, the room was overstuffed with settees, armoires, secretaries, little desks, footstools and the like. Hodding could have opened an antique store on the inventory in that room alone.

"We're not going to find anything in here," Elsabeth said despairingly. "Not even if we had all night."

Briggs was inclined to agree. As much as he hated to admit it, it was beginning to seem more and more as though they were on a wild-goose chase. They'd seen Hodding and they'd seen how he lived, but apart from that they'd accomplished nothing.

He started to say as much when Elsabeth suddenly raised her hand. "Ssh."

Footsteps were coming down the hall directly toward the room. They stopped and in the silence they heard a slight creaking. The doorknob was turning.

Briggs grabbed Elsabeth, took one quick glance around, and plunged through a door on the opposite side of the room. He had no idea where it led and didn't care. The chances were that the interlopers were just one more eager couple in search of privacy, but he wasn't going to risk it.

The door he picked led not, as he had hoped, to a bath, which would have had a window and thereby a chance at escape, but into darkness smelling of cedar. A closet. He cursed under his breath. They were out of sight and safe for the moment, but they were also trapped.

Voices were coming from the bedroom. They could hear two men talking. In the faint light from under the door, Elsabeth's face was pale and strained. Briggs put his arm around her gently, as together they listened.

"I don't care what happened," one of the men said angrily. "I gave you an order and I expected it to be carried out. Instead you made a complete mess of it. A moron could have done better.''

The other man muttered something indistinct, which prompted an even angrier outburst. ''I don't pay you for excuses! The woman should have been dealt with days ago. That was child's play. Instead you manage to be caught and arrested. Do you know what it cost me to get you out? Do you have any idea?''

''Yeah, boss, I know, but—''

''But nothing. First Dickinson, then the botched job with the woman, then Ruglio, then that godawful mess at the warehouse. What exactly am I paying you for, Charles? Would you mind telling me that?''

''It's not as simple as you think, boss. The woman had better protection than we thought. Geez, that guy came at me like a tank. And then there's that creepy house she lives in, we didn't figure on that. You know what happened to Mick, he's still not himself, lemme tell you. Down in the basement, he swears he saw something before he passed out. He says—''

''Shut up,'' Hodding ordered. ''Don't insult my intelligence. Mick will be fine, he had a little shock, that's all. Besides, you were in charge. It was *your* idea to grab the cop, *your* idea to work him over, *your* idea to go after the woman, and it was you who let them both get away.''

''I didn't *let!* That's not how it was. You weren't there. I'm tellin' you, all hell broke loose! It was like something out of a horror movie. This awful music blaring at us and that smoke grabbing at our throats and...''

''Silence! I have reached the limit of my patience. In case you haven't noticed, I have guests in the house this evening. *Important* guests. I do not have time to listen to your whining. You will keep out of sight until they have left and then I will tell you how I expect you to rectify the damage you've done. Is that clear?''

Chumpster muttered under his breath in a way Hodding took for assent. ''Very well, then. I have a final meeting with President Selim next month and Comrade Chi Liu has almost finalized his requirements. Nothing, I repeat *nothing* can be allowed to get in the way of my completing those deals. Do you understand?''

''Yeah, boss.''

''No more trouble, Charles. One more mistake and you join Ruglio. He got ideas above his station and he paid for them. Don't you forget that.''

''Ruglio wouldn't have really talked, boss. He was just spouting off, is all.''

''Oh, really? What a shame, then, since he's dead. Keep in mind, Charles, that I am a patient and forgiving man, but I do have my limits.''

''Yeah, boss.''

''Stay in here and keep the door locked. I must rejoin my guests.''

''Whatever you say, boss.''

The door opened and shut again. There was a click as Chumpster turned the key in the lock. Briggs and Elsabeth looked at each other. They could hear Chumpster moving around in the room, muttering to himself. He didn't sound too happy.

They could stay in the closet for a while. Heck, it was so big, a family of twelve could have lived in it. But there was no guarantee Chumpster wouldn't decide to explore. It might dawn on his little pea brain that he ought to try to get something solid on his boss that didn't also implicate him, and that Hodding had inadvertently provided him with the perfect opportunity to do so.

An angry and undoubtedly well-armed Chumpster was something Briggs didn't really want to confront, at least not while trapped in a closet. He was trying to figure a way out when Elsabeth bent down near the floor. There was a small space between it and the bottom of the closet door. Her hand moved—Briggs was never sure how or where—and a tendril of mauve smoke fluttered past his nose. Most of it, he quickly realized, was headed in the opposite direction, out into the bedroom.

A couple of seconds passed before Chumpster reacted. He uttered a strangled cry, which was followed by a crash as he backed into a small and most assuredly delicate piece of furniture, turning it into splinters. "Oh, geez, not again!"

"Come on," Elsabeth said. They burst out of the closet and across the room. Chumpster was huddled in one corner, batting with both hands at the smoke. He started as they went past him, but made no attempt to follow.

The door was locked but the key was still in the lock. Briggs grabbed it and jerked the door open, thrusting Elsabeth into the hall. He followed, slamming and locking the door behind them. They were halfway down the corridor before they heard Chumpster pounding on the door and howling.

The noise attracted the attention of two burly security guards who had come up to the second floor. They tensed and reached inside their jackets.

Briggs didn't hang around to see what they were carrying. On a table near the stairs was an oversized silver tray with writing engraved on it—Vanderkell

Polo Club, Championship Team, 1986—something to that effect. Briggs grabbed it.

"Hold on!"

The tray hit the edge of the topmost step, Briggs and Elsabeth hit the tray, he shoved, and she screamed. The tray flew down the marble steps and around the curve on a wild toboggan ride straight to the bottom. Elsabeth hung on for dear life, hardly daring to peek. Her skirt billowed around them, making it look as though they were being propelled by a black satin cloud. They streaked across the entry hall, scattering squealing guests right and left, and flew out the entrance. The tray bounced down the stairs and finally landed with a splat next to the startled valet who looked at them bemusedly.

"Car, sir?"

"Yeah," Briggs growled. *"Pronto."*

The valet ran to oblige as Briggs hauled Elsabeth to her feet. They were only a few hundred yards away from the car but Hodding was already coming through the door with half a dozen goons behind him. Decorum had apparently been thrown to the wind. All were armed.

The guests nearest the door saw the guns and screamed. Whatever the night had been for them—glamorous, exciting or merely tiresome—its character had abruptly changed. Suddenly there was deadly danger and the unavoidable knowledge that something was terribly wrong.

Oblivious to all this or simply beyond caring, Hodding screamed, "Get them!"

"That's our cue," Briggs said. He seized Elsabeth's hand and they ran. Behind them there was a crashing in the bushes and the sound of dogs barking.

Abruptly Briggs stopped. Elsabeth started to protest but he held up a hand. "There's no way they aren't going to get us. Don't move."

Heart in mouth, she did as he said. The crashing came nearer until finally two huge German shepherds bounded into view. They stopped a few feet away and bared their teeth, growling.

Slowly, never taking his eyes from the dogs, Briggs slid a hand into his pocket. He withdrew a small vial with a spray cap.

"Hold your breath," he murmured.

Elsabeth did as he said and closed her eyes for good measure. She knew the dogs were a terrible danger but at the same time she didn't want to see them harmed. Whatever was in that vial must be an extremely powerful deterrent.

She heard the hiss of the spray, followed swiftly by canine whines. Opening her eyes, she dared a peek. Instead of the dogs being in distress as she had expected, they were running around in circles, sniffing the ground and wagging their tails enthusiastically.

Briggs waited a moment longer before he hefted the vial, still spraying, into the bushes away from them. The dogs promptly followed.

"Let's go," Briggs said. He took her hand and together they ran, not pausing until they could no longer hear the dogs.

"What was that?" Elsabeth asked when they finally stopped to catch their breaths.

"Synthetic sex hormone," Briggs said. "It reproduces the smell of female dogs in heat. The company that makes it offered a trial supply to the department. A lot of times we have to go into buildings where there are attack dogs. We'd just as soon not have to shoot them. So far it seems to work pretty well."

"I'll say," Elsabeth murmured. "But aren't those dogs going to be awfully mad when they find out they were tricked?"

"Probably. Let's not hang around to find out."

The dogs were taken care of but the guards were not. They were still crashing around, shouting to each other, and in the process, getting closer. Briggs looked around for someplace to hide. Off in the distance, serene and lovely under the moonlight, stood a greenhouse. It was in the Victorian style, made of white wrought iron embellished with curlicues and flourishes. In the shadows it appeared to float above the ground as though conjured up by a helpful hand.

The door to the greenhouse was unlocked. They went through and found themselves in a forest of tropical plants and hot, humid air. Briggs thrust the more insistent branches out of their way as they plunged further into the building. Behind them they could hear the guards close on their trail.

"Get down here," Briggs said. He pushed Elsabeth behind one of the larger trees. "Don't make a sound."

He left her and started back in the direction they'd come, apparently intending to distract their pursuers away from her.

"Like hell," Elsabeth muttered under her breath. "Somehow that man's going to get the message."

She caught up with him at the door. He turned, his face grim. "Elsabeth, I told you . . ."

"And I told you I won't be left behind. Look out!"

Briggs swung around just in time to block a blow that would have knocked him unconscious. He ducked another, came up hard and landed a right to the stomach of his assailant. Only then did he notice who it was.

Somebody had let Chumpster out.

"Great," Briggs said. "Just what I wanted, a wrestling match with a gorilla."

Chumpster frowned. "Smart guy, huh. Time you got yours." He lunged at Briggs.

They went down, fists pounding, rolling over and over on the green lawn, past the greenhouse, past a shed, all the way to—

Off in the distance, sirens sounded.

Briggs landed one more punch to Chumpster's jaw, watched his eyes rotate back in his head, and dragged him up by the shirtfront. "Hear that?"

The hit man groaned. His head lolled back. The sirens shrieked, coming steadily closer.

"Oh, geez," Chumpster groaned. He knew when he was beaten. "This time it's gonna be for real."

"You got it, buddy," Briggs said, hauling him upright.

Chumpster shook his head dazedly. "My mom's gonna be so mad. She told me...oh, geez."

Briggs stared at him. "Your mother? You have a mother?"

Chumpster's eyes cleared slightly. He looked offended. "'Course I do. Whatta ya think, I came outta some vat?"

"Could have fooled me. But what the heck, tell you what I'm going to do. You're in a tight fix right now. Hodding's going to claim everything was your idea—

Dickinson, Ruglio, everything. He's going to let you take the rap.''

"I'll turn state's evidence. I'll testify against him. He'll—''

"Hire the biggest guns that ever came out of law school to work you over. *And* while he's at it, he'll put out a contract that'll have every two-bit hood from here to Tibet gunning for you.''

Chumpster's face crumbled but he still tried to hang tough. "The Feds'll protect me. They'll have to.''

"Maybe. Or maybe they'll use you like they tried to use us." He glanced towards Elsabeth who stood off to one side observing the exchange. She was holding her skirts high off the ground and there was a funny look on her face. That would have to wait until he had time to figure it out. First things first.

"You want to be bait, Charles, or you want to—''

"What? What? Tell me?"

Briggs slipped a hand into his jacket pocket. He withdrew a small tape recorder and held it in front of Chumpster's face.

"Little present, buddy, from me to you.''

"Whaz this?'' Chumpster demanded.

"Just something I like to carry around with me. It comes in handy in closets, for instance, when creeps like Hodding are shooting their mouths off. Give it to the D.A. You'll be surprised how nice he is to you after that.''

Chumpster's face cleared. Slowly he said, "It was you in the closet, then, not—'' He broke off and looked over his shoulder to Elsabeth.

"Listen, you done me a favor so lemme give you a little advice. She's a great-looking broad but if I wuz you, I wouldn't turn my back on her.''

"I'll keep that in mind," Briggs said. Over Chumpster's shoulder, he could see a line of police officers making their way across the lawn double-time with guns drawn. He grinned and slid the tape recorder into the other man's pocket. "Time to meet your public, buddy."

Much later when Chumpster and the others had been taken away—Hodding screaming for his lawyers and Chumpster already talking a blue streak—Briggs found Elsabeth standing off to one side of the crowd. Her hair was tumbling around her shoulders, the top of her gown had slipped just a little, and she looked absolutely gorgeous.

He headed straight for her, only to have her start backing off again.

"Hey, what gives?" he demanded.

She held up her hands, laughing and backpedaling all at the same time. "You were great, Briggs, really great. My hero."

"So, what's the problem?" He was starting to feel a little hurt. After all, he had saved both their lives, beaten the bad guys *and* turned an ordinary Greenwich social event into an evening no one would ever forget. For that, a guy ought to get at least a little appreciation.

"Briggs, when you and Chumpster were going at it, you—"

"What? Don't tell me you don't like what I did? Hodding hung himself talking in the bedroom and I got it all on tape. Who better to do him in than the guy who would have taken the rap?"

"You did the right thing," Elsabeth said gently, knowing how much it had cost him to bend the law even that much. "But—"

"What? But what?"

"You rolled into a—a compost heap," she blurted out. "You and Chumpster were fighting in—"

He froze and took a sniff. The look on his face would have been funny if the smell hadn't been quite so—pungent.

"Great," Briggs said. He started to laugh himself. "I make the last and biggest bust of my career, and do I end up covered in glory? Oh, no, what I'm covered in is sh—"

"Never mind," Elsabeth interrupted crisply. "A nice, hot soak and you'll be good as new." She shook her head regretfully. "But I think the tux has had it."

"That's okay," Briggs said magnanimously. "I'll get a new one for the wedding." He started to take her hand, remembered himself and backed off. Instead he tossed her the keys to the M.G. "You go ahead. I'll get a ride."

Elsabeth caught the keys and gave him a long, smoky glance.

"I'll be waiting," was all she said.

It was enough.

Chapter 18

Briggs stretched luxuriously in the bed. The sheets were cool, the air fragrant, and he was totally at peace. He couldn't remember the last time he'd felt so relaxed, mind and body. The reception he'd gotten when he arrived at the house undoubtedly had something to do with that. He smiled as he remembered.

Elsabeth had had a bath waiting for him, steaming hot and liberally scented with sandalwood. She herself had been dressed only in a very short robe that left her long, slender legs delightfully bare. He had slipped into the tub with a heartfelt sigh that turned to a groan as she proceeded to scrub him. Half an hour and two tubfuls later, he was pronounced clean. Which was just as well since he didn't think he could have waited a moment longer to take her to bed.

Afterward, lying close together, they talked about what had happened. Most of the questions were already answered but not quite all.

"What do you suppose Chumpster meant when he talked about Mick seeing something in the basement right before he passed out?" Elsabeth asked.

Briggs frowned. "Nothing, I guess. He must have been having some kind of hallucination."

"Maybe...but it sounded as though he was awfully scared. I can't understand that."

"No," Briggs agreed. He thought for a moment, back to the day when he first saw the house and everything he'd experienced there since. "There's nothing frightening about this place. On the contrary, it's somehow—I don't know exactly—maybe friendly's the right word. It's a friendly house."

"I always thought so," Elsabeth said. "Ever since I was a little girl, I've felt especially welcomed here. A lot of that had to do with Georgette but not all of it."

Softly she added, "But Mick was terrified. Why would he have such a different reaction from the two of us?"

Briggs looked down at her. He touched a hand to her hair gently, savoring how good she felt in his arms. "Because we're different from him. Not to make too much of it, but you and I are pretty straight arrows, we try to do what's right and we don't hurt anyone. Mick's a hit man, he makes his living terrorizing people." He was silent for a moment before he asked, "Have you had a chance to read much of that book we found?"

Elsabeth nodded. "It's fascinating. Most of it's about the garden and people coming and going, and then there are the 'recipes.' I'm convinced most of them are medicinal. They ought to be checked out. We've been learning more and more that the so-called old wives' tales had a lot of truth to them."

"What else is there?"

"Not much except..."

"What?"

"I'm not sure. It's more of a feeling than anything else. After I read all the way through I just had such a sense of being close to Martha Byrnes and the people she helped. As though there were still a part of them trying to help us understand." She snuggled closer and sighed. "Martha shows such love for the earth, such reverence for nature. I think that was really the major part of their religion. She found joy in the smallest things—a flower, a bird, a breeze. That sustained her against all odds. If there is a part of her still here, I'm glad of it."

His arms tightened around her. Softly he murmured, "So am I, sweetheart."

She propped herself up on her elbow, looking down at him. Her red-gold hair drifted over them. In the dim light her eyes were fathomless. "It would be an awfully boring world if we understood everything in it, wouldn't it, Briggs?"

He was very tired, almost on the edge of sleep, but he sensed she was asking him something important. "Sure would," he murmured. "Be awfully boring... without things to wonder about."

She sighed again and settled back against him. Her lips curved in a smile as her hand lightly stroked his chest, savoring the strength and reassurance of this man she had chosen as her own.

Briggs smiled, too, in his sleep. He did not see the tiny wisp of mauve and lavender smoke drifting out the window, upward into the twilight, higher and higher to where the wind murmurs ancient secrets.

* * * * *

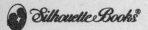

SILHOUETTE·INTIMATE·MOMENTS®

IT'S TIME TO MEET
THE MARSHALLS!

In 1986, bestselling author Kristin James wrote A VERY SPECIAL FAVOR for the Silhouette Intimate Moments line. Hero Adam Marshall quickly became a reader favorite, and ever since then, readers have been asking for the stories of his two brothers, Tag and James. At last your prayers have been answered!

In August, look for THE LETTER OF THE LAW (IM #393), James Marshall's story. If you missed youngest brother Tag's story, SALT OF THE EARTH (IM #385), you can order it by following the directions below. And, as our very special favor to you, we'll be reprinting A VERY SPECIAL FAVOR this September. Look for it in special displays wherever you buy books.

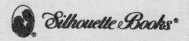
Silhouette Books®

You'll flip . . . your pages won't!
Read paperbacks *hands-free* with

Book Mate • I

The perfect "mate" for all your romance paperbacks
Traveling • Vacationing • At Work • In Bed • Studying
• Cooking • Eating

Perfect size for all standard paperbacks, this wonderful invention makes reading a pure pleasure! Ingenious design holds paperback books OPEN and FLAT so even wind can't ruffle pages – leaves your hands free to do other things. Reinforced, wipe-clean vinyl-covered holder flexes to let you turn pages without undoing the strap . . . supports paperbacks so well, they have the strength of hardcovers!

Pages turn WITHOUT opening the strap.

SEE-THROUGH STRAP

Reinforced back stays flat.

Built in bookmark

BOOK MARK

BACK COVER HOLDING STRIP

10" x 7¼" . opened.
Snaps closed for easy carrying. too.